BISHOP 3

A NOVEL

FALL FROM GRACE

AWARD-WINNING AUTHOR OF THE *"KEEPING THE SECRET"* TRILOGY

RM JOHNSON

Good Read!!
or
Finished
10/23/20

Bishop 3

RM Johnson

BISHOP 3
FALL FROM GRACE
RM JOHNSON

Marcusarts LLC—Atlanta, GA

1

Larry Lakes sat slumped, his head lowered, his face bleeding, lip busted, left eye swelling, his wrists cuffed to a metal table.

After being dragged into the police station, thrown and locked in a cell, three officers severely beat him, one of which was Officer Bonner— Mayor Richard Bonner's son. He was the officer that pulled Larry and Shreeva over hours ago.

He and the other white officer, Miller, were the men that planted the three pounds of cocaine in the trunk of Larry's car and said that it was his.

The bright overhead light of the holding room shining down on his shoulders, Larry opened his swelling eyes to see another drop of blood hit the table he was chained to.

The cops falsely accused him of having those drugs, of attempting to sell them, increasing the sentence he would receive if found guilty. It was retaliation for the last offense against Mayor Bonner in the war he and Larry were entangled in.

Bonner beat and raped Larry's mistress, Shreeva, when she would not agree to continue sleeping with the mayor. For putting his hands on her Larry determined Mayor Bonner needed to be taught a lesson.

Accompanied by Tyrell Suggs, Larry paid Mayor Bonner a visit at his home.

When the front door was answered, Tyrell Suggs grabbed the mayor's wife by the hair, and forced her to lead them to Bonner's office. Inside that office Larry informed Bonner of how grave of a mistake he had made.

"I'm going to show you what it feels like to not be able to protect the woman you love."

Bonner, a big man with a big belly, sat behind his desk in a white undershirt and suit slacks, gasping when he saw Tyrell Suggs pull out a gun and press it to Mrs. Bonner's head. He told the woman to drop to her knees and suck his dick. And after the deed was done Larry told Mrs. Bonner to scoop up and lick what was ejaculated on her face and the front of her shirt.

As Mrs. Bonner was doing as she was told, bawling, sucking the come from her fingers, the thick white fluid dripping from her chin, Mayor Bonner threatened Larry, telling him he would pay for what was happening. But Larry wasn't concerned about the fat man's threats. The hidden cameras Shreeva had mounted throughout her condo had Mayor Bonner on tape sexually assaulting her. Larry made that clear to Bonner; the man was well aware of the insurance Larry had against him. And that was the reason Larry was shocked when he saw the officer that had arrested him was Bonner's son.

All the way to the station—stuffed and cuffed in the back seat of the police cruiser—Larry warned the junior Bonner through the steal security grate.

"This is a mistake, son. Take me back now and I might consider not filing false imprisonment charges against you and your father."

"Shut the fuck up, child molester, or you'll get a worse beating than you're already gonna get at the station!" Officer Bonner shouted over his shoulder.

And the beating Larry had gotten once inside the station had been an agonizing one.

After he had been assaulted, Larry was dragged into the interrogation room where he presently sat. Bleeding from his mouth, the room spinning around him, Larry heard himself softly say, "I want my lawyer."

"Yeah, whatever," one of the cops standing nearby said.

Larry lifted his head to look the officer in the face then raised his voice as loud as he dared. "I want my fucking lawyer!"

Surprisingly, the cop looked as though he understood the consequences of withholding Larry's rights to his attorney. "Someone will bring you a phone."

Larry didn't know just how long that took. He figured he was blacking in and out, but he wasn't sure. He thought he remembered squinting down at a phone, the numbers blurring as he dialed his lawyer, Walter Watts. He believed he spoke to him, told Walter the travesty that was taking place, but that all could've been a dream.

Moments later, Larry thought he blacked in to hear a familiar voice. Again, he raised his head off the cold table, a pool of blood and saliva left on its metal surface. Mayor Bonner stood in front of him smiling, his huge belly buttoned up in a large suit jacket as though it was 9 A.M. when Larry knew it was closer to three in the morning.

Bonner paced, his hands clasped behind his back, shaking his head. "Mmm, mmm, mmm! We all knew you were a child molesting, pervert, Bishop Lakes, but who knew you were also a drug dealer."

"Those...those aren't my drugs." Larry heard the words warble from his mouth. His lips were swollen. His jaw hurt like hell.

"But my son found them in your car," Bonner said. "His partner, Officer Miller corroborates that fact." Bonner stooped down, set a forearm on the edge of the table, very near Larry's face, and stared in Larry's whirling eyes. "Who do you think a jury will believe? Two upstanding police officers, one of which happens to be the mayor's son, or a drug slinging, baby chaser?"

"I told you! Those...aren't my drugs!"

Bonner smiled. "That's what they all say."

Larry angrily lunged at him, but was snatched back by his cuffs like a raging guard dog held by a chain.

"Such a violent man," Bonner said, wagging a finger. "Maybe if you hadn't such a temper you wouldn't be in this situation."

"You need to let me go," Larry said, resting his cuffed wrists in his lap, laying his head back on the table. He was exhausted and in considerable pain. "Just let me go."

"Maybe there's a way that can happen," Bonner suggested.

Larry rose up in his seat, only seeing the man out of one eye now, for the other was completely shut. "How?"

"The church you've built in my city. The church you know none of my people want there. If you agree to—"

Bonner was interrupted by the interrogation room door flying open, banging against the wall behind it.

"Don't you say another word to my client," Larry's attorney, Walter Watts said. "And Bishop, you don't have to say anything else to this man."

Larry dropped the side of his face on the table once more, listening as Walter scolded Bonner, suddenly stopping mid-sentence after taking a look at Larry.

"What the hell happened to my client?"

Larry felt Walter's arm around him, heard his voice louder in his ear. "Bishop! What did they do to you?"

Larry heard nothing else, for once again, he blacked out.

When he woke, he was still in the interrogation room, still chained to the table. Walter was in front of him, holding a small plastic cup and two pills.

"Take these. It's ibuprofen. It's all they had, but it should help a little."

Larry took the pills and struggled to reach the cup to his mouth, insisting on doing it himself when Walter reached out and offered to help.

"How long...how long was I out?"

"Twenty minutes. I thought to wake you, but I figured you needed the rest."

"What's going on, Walter?" Larry asked, worried that his situation was worse than he initially thought, considering he was still sitting there cuffed and yet to be released.

"I spoke to Mayor Bonner. For some reason he seems to be the one in charge of this, not the police captain or any of the detectives."

Larry knew the reason why. "Those aren't my drugs, Walter."

"I know, but Bonner believes they are and he intends to go after you hard, lock you up for the full ten years allowed for the charge of possession with intent to distribute."

"But I told you—"

"I know, Bishop. You and Bonner have your differences. You don't like each other. I don't know what you did to the man to have him go to these lengths to get back at you, but I figured that's what he's doing. I asked him if there was any way we could make these charges disappear, figuring he's setting you up to get something else."

"And?"

"You already know, Bishop. The new church you built in Union City. Bonner wants it."

2

Larry waited anxiously for Shreeva to pick up the phone.

After Walter told Larry that Bonner wanted the church, Larry figured the man must've bumped his head and forgotten about the evidence Larry and Shreeva had against him. Yes, Bonner and Bonner's son would say that those drugs were Larry's, but when Larry threatened to give that video of the mayor raping Shreeva to the media, have it aired all over the country, he was sure Bonner would think again about his position.

"Give him my church?" Larry said. He would've laughed at the idea if his face hadn't been hurting so badly. "Go back and tell Bonner that if he wants to play this game, we can play it. Tell him I still have that little something that—"

"Bishop," Walter interrupted. "The Mayor told me you'd say something like that, and if you did, tell you that your lady friend, Shreeva Jackson was released, taken home by the arresting officers, walked into her place, and they even checked it out to make sure there was nothing there that shouldn't have been."

"What are you talking about?" Larry said, trying to yank his hands free of the cuffs. "What does that mean?"

"I don't know, Bishop. That was just what the mayor wanted me to tell you. He said you would be allowed to call her if you like to make sure she's all right."

Walter produced his phone and gave it to Larry.

Now Larry waited for Shreeva to pick up.

"Are you all right?" he asked, panicking, when she finally answered the phone.

"Yes," Shreeva said, sounding scared and out of breath. "But—"

"But what?"

Desperation in her voice, Shreeva said, "They took it, Larry. They pushed me in here, threw me around and threatened to do much worse unless I gave them the video. I'm sorry. I tried not to, but after one of them slapped me, I just didn't want to go through that—"

"No, no. Don't apologize," Larry said, feeling beaten and foolish for never taking the video from Shreeva. "Are you sure you're okay?"

"Yes. Yes."

Despite what she said, Larry could hear that she was crying.

"How about you. They didn't hurt—"

"I'm fine," Larry said. "Everything is fine. I'll be home shortly," he said, looking up at Walter. "Don't you worry, and get some sleep. Love you." Larry sadly disconnected the call, and handed it back to Walter.

"What was that about?" Walter asked, concern wrinkling his already aging face.

"Nothing," Larry said, leaning back in the metal chair, knowing that with the theft of his only insurance against Bonner, he was left defenseless. There was nothing left for him to do, but cooperate. "If you would, Walter, tell Mayor Bonner we can talk now."

3

Physically spent, Marian shuddered against the aftershocks of a third monumental orgasm. Her legs trembling, nails digging into Paul's back, she tried to force herself away from him. Paul would not release his hold on her.

He was trying to get further into her head, make her fall in love with him, make it so she could not go a single moment without thinking of him.

Marian had told Paul that after the last time they made love. He laughed, kissed her lightly on the lips and turned away as though she was speaking foolishness. But Marian knew she was right about him.

Paul had brazenly been chasing her—despite the fact she was married—since the day he was hired as her personal assistant. Now that divorce between her and Larry was imminent, it seemed Paul had been devoting all of his energy to finally getting the woman he had been so desperately pursuing.

"What's on your mind? Something bothering you?" Paul asked Marian last night, before they made love.

She shook her head. "I'm fine. Just feel a little bit of a headache coming on," she lied. Her mind was still on the video she had found of her husband abusing those boys, and the confrontation she had with him after that, demanding that Larry pay Urail, Robby and Van three million dollars— even though that didn't come close to what she felt they were entitled to after enduring the suffering dealt to them by Larry.

For the last several months, there were rumors and there were accusations made about her husband, accusations that were proven false, only confirming that Larry was the righteous man he had always claimed to be. But the video proved otherwise. It proved that Marian was married to a monster: a liar, a hypocrite—damn near the devil himself.

Last night looked over at Paul who was sitting in a corner chair of her bedroom, his face cupped in his hands, staring intently at her.

"I found some disturbing things," Marian finally admitted, deciding there was no reason to continue to keep it a secret. "Some horrible things that belonged to my husband."

Paul came over, sat beside Marian, wrapped his arm around her. "Tell me."

The meeting with the attorneys, the demands she made of her husband after finding out the truth about him, her impending divorce, and the fact that she was going to sell the house—she told Paul everything.

He wiped away the tear that fell down her cheek with a thumb.

"Is there anything I can do?"

"Nothing more than you've already been doing," Marian said.

Paul stayed last night, which he had been doing pretty much on the regular since Marian had gone to his place—the kids in the back seat of the truck—and told him she missed him, which led to their reconciliation.

This morning, he sat at the kitchen table between Jabari and Simone while Marian made scrambled eggs for the kids before taking them to school. She knew it was wrong to have Paul there like that. Estelle, her mother, made her aware of that fact, pulling Marian aside after the first breakfast, three mornings ago, when she saw Paul sitting at the table, laughing with the kids, as though he had every right to be there.

"And what do you think your children will think seeing that man here all times of night and in the morning?" Estelle asked her.

Marian didn't have an adequate answer for her mother. Even she knew it probably wasn't right to have Paul there so soon.

"If they have a problem with it, I'm sure they'll let me know," was all she said before turning and walking away.

After breakfast this morning, while the kids were upstairs getting dressed for school, Paul helped Marian clear the table, even though he was no longer her personal assistant and not required to do those kinds of things.

Paul had handed in his resignation almost two weeks ago, was able to tap a friend he knew who worked at the High Museum of Art and managed to land a job there.

Taking the dishes from Paul, Marian set them in the sink, lowered her head, still overcome by the newfound knowledge she had of her husband and all the fallout she knew she would have to deal with.

Finally, she felt Paul behind her, imagined him uncomfortable, not knowing what to do with his hands—whether to leave, stay, say something or remain quiet. She felt bad for putting him in that position.

Paul's hands on her shoulders, she felt him press up behind her.

"I'm coming back over tonight. I've been doing some thinking, and I think we need to talk about what you're gonna do."

Marian opened her eyes, wanting to ask him what made him think he had any say in what her future would be. Instead she turned to him, nodded her head and softly said "I'll see you tonight, then."

Now, after making love, Marian's body finally coming down from the orgasms Paul had given her, she kissed his lips, watching as he smiled confidently at the fact her body responded so wonderfully, so completely to his touch.

17

"I take it that you're satisfied." He chuckled.

"Shut up, boy," Marian said, turning her face away, playfully pushing him in the chest. "Get off me."

Paul rose, climbed out of bed, and from the candlelight flickering on her dresser, Marian admired the man's taught body—the way his muscles smoothly contracted and expanded in his back when he walked.

She stretched out in bed, a content smile on her face despite the turmoil she endured most of the day, thankful that "the talk" Paul spoke of having this morning never happened. She had been dreading it all day, wondering what lines he might cross, how he might try to insert himself into her life and the lives of her children. It was a discussion she just really didn't need to have at that moment.

Marian heard the water in the bathroom cut off, saw the bathroom door open and the light go out. Paul walked over, kneeled beside Marian and rested the side of his face on her bare stomach.

She rubbed her fingers over the tiny curls in his hair, thankful to have him there.

He lifted his head, kissed her belly button softly, and in the dim candle light, Marian could see that he was looking up at her.

"I have something for you," he said, taking hold of her hand. Before Marian could ask what that something was, she felt him slipping a ring onto her finger.

"I know everything is messed up right now, but I want you to marry me." There was a light, joking tone in his voice, but she felt he was deadly serious.

Marian lifted her hand over her face, looked up at the ring. Compared to the four-karat job she paraded around with for the last decade—the diamond that blinded everyone—this one, Marian could barely see. But that didn't matter. It wasn't about the ring, but the man who presented it, and this man just happened to be a very good one.

"Paul—" Marian started.

"I'm not saying we get married tomorrow—even if you could, which I know you can't. I'm not saying we even do it in a year, but if you say yes, we can still be engaged. I can be here, live with you, be in your kid's lives and not have your mother looking over the table at me like she's going to kill me in my sleep."

Marian chuckled aloud, unable to help it, but she didn't want Paul to think she'd actually say yes to the lunacy he was presenting.

Paul continued—"I think we have a good thing going. It's still new, I know, but it's good. I think we should do this. I think it'll be good for the kids, for you and for me. And if ever it's not working out the way you want, you can tell me to get out and I won't even give you a hard time about why. So?" Paul said, tightening his grip around Marian's hand. "Will you get engaged to—"

"Yes," Marian said, not giving herself time to think, time to rationalize why it made zero sense to agree to this—time to back out. She decided on emotion and nothing else. Did having Paul in her life feel good? Yes. Did the kids like him? Yes. Unlike her husband, could she trust him? Yes. Did she actually believe they could work, that they might spend the rest of the their lives together? Hmmm, maybe. But none of that really even mattered. Right now, he was there for her, and right now she needed him there. If it took agreeing to get engaged to keep him there, then so be it.

"Yes, Paul. I'll get engaged to you."

4

Larry walked into Shreeva's condo a little after five in the morning.

The entire drive home, Walter insisted that Larry go to the emergency room to get his wounds looked at.

"I'm fine," Larry said, slumped in the front seat of Walter's car. His face still

ached, but he knew nothing was broken, and he believed there were no lacerations deep enough to require stiches. "I'll patch myself up when I get home."

When he did walk into Shreeva's condo, he wasn't surprised to see that she wasn't in bed as he ordered, but wearing a robe over a nightgown, standing at one of the floor to ceiling windows, staring out at the downtown lights, her arms wrapped tightly around herself.

When Larry closed the door, Shreeva ran to him, threw her arms around him as though she hadn't seen him in years.

"I'm so sorry," she apologized, squeezing him. "I didn't want to give them the video, but they — "

Larry pulled her arms from around his neck.

Whens she caught sight of him, the damage done to his face, she cried out as though she had been the one beaten. Larry attempted to tell her the wounds weren't bad, that they didn't hurt, but she insisted they go to the hospital. When Larry strongly objected, she sat him down in the bathroom, worked on his wounds with a bottle of alcohol, hydrogen peroxide, gauze, and medical tape as though she had years of training as nurse. As she worked, she apologized profusely for allowing the officer to take the video.

"I told you I understand. Everything will be fine," Larry kept telling her. But that was a lie. After he had received word from Shreeva that Bonner had the video, Larry thought long and hard how not to give up the new church, while Bonner paced in front of him, but Larry could think of nothing that would make the drug charges disappear other than giving Bonner what he asked for.

"Are you sure you really want to blackmail me like this," Larry said to Bonner.

"I don't know what you're talking about, Bishop," Bonner said. "There is no blackmail. Those drugs are yours. But because I'm a nice man, I'm willing to extend this offer to you. But you need to give me an answer this very minute."

Saying no to the man would allow Larry to keep the church, but there was a good chance he'd be locked away behind bars.

Moments before Bonner walked in, Larry consulted with his attorney.

"Can they make these charges stick, Walter?"

"I don't think so," Walter said. "I'm sure I can prove that they planted them on you—that all this is a set-up, but Bonner intends to take this all the way to trial if he must. We'll be dealing with a jury. There's no telling how that might go with your controversial past. You lose, you could be spending the next decade in jail."

It wasn't a chance Larry could take.

"Fine Mayor Bonner," Larry said. "Drop these charges and the Union City church is yours."

Over the last fifteen minutes, while Shreeva did her best to bandage Larry's face, he explained all of that to her.

"So you had to give it up? The church?" she asked, screwing the cap on the bottle of hydrogen peroxide.

"It was the only way I could stay out of jail," Larry said, still trying to convince himself he made the right decision. "I have nothing now. No family, no church, no congregation and no home."

He lowered his face, shamefully, so tired he thought he might fall to the floor. Before he could, Shreeva's arms were around him, holding up him.

"Don't you ever say that, Daddy. You have a home right here. This place is yours as much as it is mine. What happened tonight, those cops pulling us over was a terrible thing, but don't you dare let that soil what happened before. You got down on one knee and proposed to me. I am your future wife. I am your family, and I will be here for you in every way I must, in whatever way you need. You understand me?"

Larry shook his head, turned away from Shreeva, overcome with grief.

"No!" Shreeva said, gently turning his face back to her. "We won't let this break you. I won't! You are a strong man, a good man, a man of God, and He would never give you anything you and I together can't bare."

"Fine," Larry said, under his breath, no sincerity in the statement.

"I am devoted to you, Larry. We will get through this, but I need for you to believe it as much as I do. Will you do that for me?"

Still staring in her eyes, his own, glossy with impending tears. "I will."

5

The next day, Larry stood in front of the mansion he had once lived in with his wife and children. He had not been there since Marian confronted him about the videos she found in his office safe, and in that time, there had been a FOR SALE sign posted out in front of the Union City church—the church Mayor Bonner now owned.

Larry had heard Holy Sweet Spirit, where he used to preach, now had a new pastor. He found it odd that instead of promoting someone under Larry, the board members chose to bring in someone, not only from another church, but a pastor from another state. He was a younger black man, and from what Larry heard, he was doing a good job, which made Larry angry and jealous that he wasn't missed more.

Looking up at his house, Marian's Lexus truck parked in the circular driveway, Larry noticed there was a FOR SALE sign planted in his front yard as well.

He remembered his wife saying something about not wanting to live in the filthy house anymore, and possibly putting it up for sale to help pay the boys he molested the money that was rightly owed them.

Larry walked across the driveway, his fists clenched, at the same time trying to calm himself, not wanting to lose control when he saw his wife.

Stepping up to the door, he rang the bell. A moment later, Marian opened the door, gasping, stepping back, shocked to see him.

"What…what are you doing here?"

"I want to see my children."

It was late, some time past six. Larry knew they had been home from school long ago.

"You can't. They aren't here. Even if—"

"They are!" Larry said. " Don't lie to me."

"If they were here," Marian continued. "I wouldn't let you see them. Once the divorce is final, I'll have custody of them. You won't be able to see them then, so you sure as hell can't see them now."

His hand knotted into even tighter fists now, Larry attempted to look over Marian's shoulder for his children. When he didn't see them, he yelled into the house, "Jabari! Simone! Jabari, it's your father!"

"Stop that!" Marian shouted. "They aren't here, I told you!"

Larry focused his attention on his wife, stared at her angrily. "You can't keep my children from me like this forever. I want to see my son."

"Why, so you can fuck him up the ass like you did those poor boys?"

That was the straw that Marian had been bending since she opened the door. She finally fucking broke it. Slapping both his hands onto the front of her shirt, Larry snatched Marian out of the doorway, slammed her against the house beside the door, and shoved a hand into her throat, clamping down.

"Do you know who you're talking—"

Before he could finish his statement, Larry felt an anvil hammering him in between the legs. It was Marian's knee, sending the most excruciating pain Larry, dropping him in front of her, to his hands and knees.

Crying out, he heard Marian scrambling away from him, both front doors slamming closed, leaving him there, rolling on his side, both his arms rapped around his belly to suffer.

6

Inside a small bar, music pounding so hard the walls and floor vibrated, Larry downed what had to have been his fifth shot of tequila. Flashing rainbow-colored lights refracted off a huge mirrored disco ball in the center of the bar as scores of men, some shirtless, some bottomless— wearing nothing but boy shorts or thongs—danced and jumped about the floor.

Larry's vision blurring, he squinted, forcing together the two images of his old friend Dennard Curry.

Dennard, a famous black attorney to some of Atlanta's biggest reality TV stars and athletes, was the man Larry went to for advice on just how to handle the boys and the settlement meeting. After losing everything, Larry needed a friend to hang out with, to talk to, and to get so fucked up with that nothing else mattered.

When Larry called Dennard an hour ago, after the terrible meeting with Marian, the man picked up the phone, his voice filled with sympathy. "I heard what happened with the police. Those crooked motherfuckers!"

"How did you—"

"Word gets out, Larry. But it stays within the inside circle. Only the connected people know. This stuff never makes it's way out to the public. You okay?"

Larry didn't answer, figuring Dennard knew the answer.

"Where are you? Let me pick you up. I know exactly what you need," Dennard said.

They ended up at a gay bar supposedly only the most connected men knew about.

"No one you know will be here," Dennard said, as they walked up to the building with blacked out windows and no signage. Heavy bass escaped the windowless door that opened and closed, flashing glimpses of the red light that illuminated the club. "You can relax and do whatever you need to do here without anyone in your business," Dennard said, pulling the door and holding it open for Larry.

Larry stepped in, almost missing the fact that he no longer had to look over his shoulder, had to worry about people spotting him in places like this. He had nothing to lose now.

"How are you feeling?" Dennard shouted at Larry from the barstool beside him. Dennard wore a heavy net tank top, his carved muscles and dark nipples plainly exposed for everyone to see.

"I'm cool," Larry said over the music. And even though he was drunk, he still could not rid himself of the horrible fight he had with Marian earlier.

Dennard stepped off his stool, leaned over, cupped a hand around Larry's ear, and said, "You aren't cool. I can tell you're still bothered by what happened." He placed an arm around Larry's shoulder, coaxed him around. "See that man over there?"

Larry's eyes followed the direction Dennard pointed to see a slender, light skinned man wearing a pink Mohawk and leather chaps, his bare ass hanging out the back. He danced cooly beside the men's bathroom door, sipping from a drink, a pink paper umbrella sticking up out the side of it.

"That man there is a very good friend of mine," Dennard said.

Larry felt his friend's lips brush against his ear, his breath warm and wet.

"And I think he has something that'll make you forget all about what's bothering you."

Fifteen minutes later, Larry stood in the stall of the men's bathroom, staring down at the back of Dennard's friend's pink Mohawk, as he relentlessly pounded the man from behind, taking all his anger and frustrations out on him.

After Dennard had pointed him out, he waved an arm, catching the man's attention,

curling a finger at him, calling him over.

The man with the black leather chaps sauntered over.

Dennard kissed him on both cheeks, whispered something in his ear, then Denard's friend extended one of his big hands to Larry.

Larry wobbled a little on his feet, looked down at the man's hand, noticing white polish on his fingernails.

"My name is Jayteesh!"

Larry shook his head, and felt Jayteesh urging him forward.

"Go with him," Denard said. "It'll be cool."

Larry allowed himself to be led through the throng of dancing men. Groped and fondled a couple of times on his way, he was too drunk and burdened to care.

Not two minutes after Jayteesh locked himself and Larry in the men's room, Larry opened his eyes after fading in and out to see Jayteesh standing over the sink, very carefully heating the curved bottom of a bent and blackened tablespoon.

Jayteesh set the tablespoon on the edge of the sink then grabbed the syringe he was holding in his teeth. He stuck the needle tip into what Larry thought was a wet cotton ball in the center of the spoon. He pulled back on the syringe's plunger, sucking fluid into the needle, squirted just a bit out of it—a thin stream of clear fluid shooting into the air.

"You ready for this, baby?" Jayteesh looked down at Larry's right arm. There was a rubber tourniquet tied just above his bicep. The vein in the bend of his elbow pulsed thick with blood. Larry had no idea how or when it was tied there.

Larry shook his head. "I don't do that stuff...no more."

Back when Larry's father had him prostituting, sucking off men in the back seats of their cars—renting Larry out for days to be abused any way the paying client felt, only to come home and have Larry's own father take a turn on him—using heroin was all Larry could do to stop from killing himself.

"No," Larry whispered, raising a weak hand, attempting to push Jayteesh away.

"Dennard told me a little bit about what you went through. That, on top of all the stuff I seen you dealing with on the news, makes me think can use a little of this." Jayteesh grabbed Larry by the arm, held his fist, and smacked the inflated vein in the bend of Larry's elbow.

Larry thought about the horrors he had to endure back then to finally get himself off that drug, but he also remembered how wonderful it made him feel when he was using. It was as if the world's problems, all the pain and torment he suffered lifted from him when he was high.

"No," Larry heard himself utter again as he saw the blurry image of Jayteesh about to introduce the needle into his arm.

A dainty gold hoop ring hanging from Jayteesh's nostrils, he stared down at Larry.

"You sure?" He pulled the needle away. "If you don't want it, I don't have to give it to you."

Larry thought about his kids, about his wife. He thought about all he had lost, all that he would never have again. He wondered how he would deal with all that, and decided there was no possible way he could. Not by himself.

"Give it to me," Larry said, then winced when he felt the bee-sting like prick of the needle, felt the veins in his arm freeze as the drug traveled up into his system, every nerve in his body catching fire as the heroin took it's course.

Larry's skull fell back against the wall, his eyes rolling around in his head, then falling closed.

7

It was the wrong thing to do, Marian thought, watching her mother, Estelle load the gun they went out and purchased not an hour ago.

Yesterday, after the incident with Larry, Marian couldn't hide how messed up in the head she was about it. Thankfully, the kids weren't able to detect her confusion about what had happened while she ate dinner with them. But after the kids had gone up stairs and went to bed, Estelle had a seat in one of the kitchen chairs while Marian washed dishes.

She hadn't heard her mother enter, and when Marian turned around, she was so startled a saucer fell from her hand and broke on the kitchen floor.

Stooping down to retrieve the big jagged sections of the plate, Marian stared in her mother's eyes, Estelle having bent down to help her.

"What's wrong with you child?"

"What are you talking about Mom," Marian said, stacking the pieces of broken glass in her hands.

"This dish?"

"It soapy. It's slipped out of my hands. It was a mistake."

"Then why are hands shaking like that?"

After the mess was cleaned up, Marian sat at the kitchen table, her legs crossed, rocking nervously in her chair. A cup of tea Estelle made her, sat on a saucer in front of Marian—something meant to calm her nerves.

"And you said he was here, that he put his hands on you?" Estelle asked. She had pulled her chair out from under the table and had it facing Marian so close that hers and Estelle's knees practically touched.

Marian nodded her head. "He said he wanted to see the kids and…yeah, he had me around the throat. I…I didn't know what he was going to do to me."

Estelle pushed back from the chair, the feet skidding loudly against the floor. "And you're walking around her like this bothers you."

"It does!"

"Like you're surprised he did this. He put his hands on you before. I seen it, walked in on the middle of it. Dammit, Marian! Why are you surprised he'd try that again, especially after you seen what he was capable of with those boys. Now that you're taking his children from him, what did you expect he'd do?"

Marian dropped her face in her hands. "I just…I…"

"Everything he has, you're threatening to take from him. You have no idea what he might do now."

Looking up, Marian brushed the hair out of her face. "So, what? Call the police, file a restraining order?"

"We can do that," Estelle said, as though she didn't have much trust in that measure. "But there's something that needs to be done first thing tomorrow morning."

That thing was going to the gun shop.

Estelle didn't tell Marian that was the destination until they pulled into the small storefront parking lot.

"What are we doing at a gun store, Mom?" Marian said, feeling betrayed. "I'm not getting a gun."

"Fine," Estelle said, shifting Marian's Lexus into PARK. "Then I'll get it."

"You already have one. Isn't one enough?"

31

"That gun is mine." Estelle pushed open the door, grabbed her purse and stepped out the truck. "You need to have your own, just in case that bastard comes back and I'm not there. Now come on," Estelle said, slamming the door.

Now, a couple of hours later, Marian still could not get used to the sight of her mother handling the gun—a 9mm. Marian shook her head, frowning, hugging herself as if afraid the weapon would do her harm.

"Take it," Estelle said.

Marian stepped back.

"Take it, girl!"

Marian took the gun. The man who sold it to them—a big white guy with a "Duck Dynasty" beard and American flag bandana wrapped around his head—taught Marian how to hold it, and how to shoot it.

"Now what?" Marian asked Estelle, holding the gun pointing toward the floor, her finger off the trigger like she was taught.

"Just want you used to holding it, not afraid of it, just in case."

"I'll always be afraid of it. And what if Simone finds it?"

"You know you don't have to worry about Simone snooping around your room."

"And Jabari," Marian said, knowing how inquisitive her son was. "What if he finds it?"

"Hide it where he won't."

Marian stared at her mother, not certain about the gun, about whether she would have the courage to fire it, even if Larry threatened her or her family again.

Estelle, obviously sensing her daughter's doubt, said, "Would you rather be frightened that the gun is in your closet, or would you prefer, when Larry comes back and he's trying to do God knows what to you and your family, you have no way to protect yourself?"

Marian thought about what was just said, not liking the visuals that accompanied that thought.

"Fine, Mom. I'll keep the gun."

8

On a daily basis, Larry did nothing but lay around Shreeva's condo, and earned nothing. His bank account had been depleted, considering he no longer had a job, and just about all of his assets were being liquidated in order to come up with the money Marian was forcing him to the pay to the boys.

On more than one occasion, Shreeva asked him if he needed any cash.

Larry had to stop himself from being offended by the gesture, Shreeva stepping to him like he was a child needing pocket change for lunch. All she was doing was trying to help him, he told himself, and sadly, he needed that help. Still, he turned the money down.

"There's nothing to be ashamed of," Shreeva said. She stood in front of him, digging in her purse, wearing a simple red dress that clung to her curvaceous figure—tight around the hips, ass and breasts. She was the hostess at a hotel restaurant. And dressing like that, like she always dressed, Larry knew the men there wouldn't be able to keep their eyes off of her, couldn't restrain themselves from approaching her, offering to take care of her in exchange for the privilege of bedding her.

That had always been the case, and Larry had never worried about the woman straying, but that was because he was caring for her.

The condo she owned, Larry bought her. The Infiniti she drove, almost all of the clothes that had those men turning their heads, Larry bought for Shreeva. But now he had nothing to offer her but himself, and that made him feel as though he could've been easily traded in. Now he was nothing more than a burden.

"I'm not ashamed," Larry said. "I just don't need your money. I'm still a man and I can still take care of myself."

Shreeva smiled like she would at a child she thought was cute.

Larry took offense to that too, but tried to hide it.

"I know you can, baby," Shreeva said, pulling a fifty dollar bill from her purse, folding it and slipping it into his palm as though keeping it from the eyes of some onlooker who might object. She kissed his lips. "I gotta go before I'm late. What do you got planned today?"

"I don't know," he grumbled, feeling guilty about the money he had taken.

Later that afternoon, Larry sat in Tyrell Suggs's living room. The man kept a home—a small three-bedroom place—he meticulously kept in Atlanta's West End.

They sat, the front door open, a gentle breeze blowing in through the screen door as Tyrell Suggs pulled from a blunt he had rolled, then offered it to Larry. It was something they used to do together before Larry became a pastor, before he met Marian, before he became legitimate. But all that was gone now. Even if someone found him using drugs again, it wouldn't make a shit's bit of difference.

Larry took the blunt, took a drag from it and held the smoke in.

"What are we gonna do about Bonner?" Tyrell Suggs said. "You know the man has to pay for that shit he did to you."

"No." Larry blew the smoke out of his mouth, letting it seep from his nostrils as he shook his head. "That's how I got here in the first place. I wasn't smart. I didn't control myself. Now I have no money, which means I can no longer pay you."

Larry felt guilty about that. Besides being his bet friend, Tyrell Suggs had been Larry's employee—more or less his personal assistant—for more than the past ten years

"It's no big deal," Tyrell Suggs said, receiving the blunt from Larry. "We hustlers. Always have been. We'll find another source soon enough."

"I think I already have," Larry said.

Out of his suit jacket pocket Larry pulled a small package, roughly the size of brick, wrapped in brown paper. He set it on the table.

An hour ago, Larry stood in the living room of a 12th floor Atlantic Station condominium, decorated elaborately with colored furniture set on top of gleaming, oak hardwood floors.

Wearing huge black Gucci sunglasses and no shirt, Jayteesh sat on the edge of an orange easy chair in the shape of a giant, open hand. The brick of heroin sat on a small round coffee table just in front of him.

"You sure you wanna do this, Bishop?" Jayteesh said, eyes covered in those shades, looking like a demented clown by the head, still wearing the pink Mohawk.

"This ain't a whole lot of weight, but consignment ain't nothing to play with. The fact we fucking aside, you still gotta come back with what you owe me on this brick. 'Bishop Larry Lakes' or not, I don't get my money, I'm gonna have to take care of you like I would any wannabe drug man."

Larry didn't appreciate the veiled threat. He was slinging drugs before Jayteesh, who appeared to be easily twenty years younger than Larry, was even born.

"I got you," Larry said. "I understand completely."

Jayteesh picked up the brick. "I'm only doing this cause your boy, Dennard, vouches for you. You know that right?" Jayteesh held out the brick to Larry. Larry stepped forward to grab it, but Jayteesh shot him a stern look and pulled the package back.

"Like I said, play with me, the shit won't end pretty for you, Bishop."

"What is it?" Tyrell Suggs said, looking down at the package Larry just set on his coffee table.

"Heroin. It's nothing we gonna do for long. But I need to make some money. *We* need to make money."

Tyrell Suggs stared at Larry, uncertainty on his face.

"If you're not sure about this, we don't—"

"It ain't me, Bishop," Tyrell Suggs assured him. "You know I'm down for whatever. You say this is what you wanna do, it's what I'm *gonna* do. I just wanna make sure you comfortable."

Again Larry considered his situation, but there wasn't anymore to think about. "Comfort has nothing to do with it, Mr. Suggs. It's what has to happen."

9

After his meeting with Tyrell Suggs, Larry found himself parked in front of the Union City church that was once his. He thought about all the work, the effort, the politicking that went into finding the funds and getting the approval to have the church built. He thought about the importance of it's existence, all those people he had told countless times about this church, all the good it would've done for his congregation.

He turned away from the structure, feeling like a liar, figuring that's how all of his former followers must've of thought of him now.

It was Mayor Bonner's fault. It was Bonner that shook Larry's hand, that Okayed the build of the church when Larry first spoke to him. With that approval, Larry sunk tens of thousands of dollars of his own money into getting the church built. Then more than half way into the erection of the building, Bonner brought those nonsensical complaints from the other church leaders about not wanting Larry in Union City, stopping the construction from going forward, he thought, slumping angrily in his car. Because of Bonner, Larry had nothing.

Having nowhere else to go, Larry went back to Shreeva's condo, walked in and set his keys on the entryway table, then fell into one of the dining room chairs. The entire way home, Larry fought the urge to steer his car in the direction of Bonner's home, kick the man's door down, and beat him till his fists were covered with the fat man's blood.

"Daddy, is that you?"

Larry heard Shreeva calling from the other room and thought if he had known that she was home, he would've gone somewhere else. All he really wanted to do was be alone in his misery at that moment.

Happy to see him, Shreeva walked over, hugged Larry around the neck, kissed his lips then leaned back to look at him. Reading the sad, disturbed expression on his face, she pouted, and spoke to him again as if talking to a child.

"Awww, not having a good day?" She said in a baby-talk voice.

"I've had better," Larry mumbled, hating when she did that.

Shreeva took his hand and attempted to pull him from his seat. "C'mon, I have somewhere I want us to go."

"Where?" Larry said, looking up, but not standing from the chair.

"It's a secret."

"Why can't you just tell me?"

"Because it wouldn't be a secret then, Daddy. C'mon," Shreeva said, pulling on his arm like a pestering child.

"I'm sorry. It's been another bad day in a week of bad days. I'm not in the mood for games," Larry said. "If you want me to even think about going with you, you gotta tell me where you're talking about."

"Fine. We're going to get marriage licenses."

"I'm not even divorced yet."

"You're still getting divorced."

"Of course I am, but—"

"And we're gonna need marriage licenses when we get married, right?" Shreeva said.

"Yeah, but—"

"Then we should go get them now, so when you are finally divorced, which I'm needing to be sooner than later, the license will be one less thing we'll have to worry about."

This was Shreeva asserting herself, her hands on her hips, her head bobbing from side to side as she made her snide comment about needing his divorce to happen sooner than later. He wasn't in the mood for any of it.

"Not today, baby," Larry said, getting up from his chair, not to go far, just somewhere she was not staring down at him.

"When did I become your trick?"

His back to her, Larry halted, then turned. "What?"

"You just dismissed me like none of what I said mattered. Like I'm not the woman you loved for more than ten years. Like I ain't the woman that stuck with your ass for all that time, doing whatever the hell you needed me to do. You dismissed me like some hoe you paying to go out on the street and sell pussy. So I'll ask again," Shreeva said with the swooping wave of a finger, one hand still on her hip. "When did I become your trick?" Shreeva said.

"Shreeva you know—"

"What I know," Shreeva interrupted. "Is that I was here before you met your wife, before there was a church and you became the big, almighty Bishop Larry Lakes. I was here," Shreeva said, stabbing a finger downward at the space in front of her. "When you were king of the hill, making millions and was the biggest shit in Atlanta, I was here. And now that all of it's gone, like you say, and nobody loves you, or respects you, or remembers the great man you were, I am still here." She stared sadly at him, wanting only to be accepted, to be loved back as much as she loved him. "I thought I wanted the first lady thing so badly, but now that I see that won't happen, it don't matter any more, because I love you, Larry."

Larry appreciated the impassioned declaration of her devotion, but it did nothing to solve his immediate problems. "It's not that easy, Shreeva."

"Dammit Larry, you just proposed. What the hell happened?"

"Me losing everything, in case you forgot. That's what happened."

Shreeva crossed her arms, nodding. "You keep saying that, even though I tell you over and over again, you still have me and I'm not nothing."

"That's not the way I meant it," Larry said.

"I know. But unless you really do wanna lose everything, you're gonna stop fussing about what you no longer have and start paying attention to what you do."

10

The next day, Larry drove an old Toyota Corolla—Tyrell Suggs's second car, for he didn't want to be recognized when he drove over to the mansion, hoping to get a glimpse of his children.

He had parked down the block, outside of the mansion's gate, for better than an hour, anticipating Marian taking the kids out to the store or something.

Almost nodding off, he perked up when he saw the Lexus truck pulling out of the gate. He quickly started the car and had been following it ever since.

Steering the car around a corner, Larry thought how Marian had been bold enough to demand sole custody of his children that night she found his videos, and even though he told her he would give her that, she had to have been crazy to believe him.

Larry had been a full-time Dad, been there for his children, cared for them as much as she did. What made her think she could just take him out of the equation, demand that he disappear and believe he'd just go?

She had another thing coming, Larry thought, following the Lexus onto 10th street, where it parked.

A bit more than a block away, he parallel parked the Toyota and lowered himself into the seat of the car, then peered over the dash, waiting to see his family.

He saw movement behind the tinted windows. Larry sat up to get a better look, then saw more than he expected.

Jabari and Simone bounded out of the truck, Marian coming around the passenger door, taking the hands of the children before they crossed the street. Then finally, out of the driver's side door of the Lexus, Paul, Marian's personal assistant, stepped down. He said something to Marian, she laughed, as did the kids, then Paul took Simone's and Marian's hand, and the four of them—like one big happy family—crossed the street and walked toward Piedmont Park.

Larry grabbed for the car door handle, pushed the door ajar, then thought twice and pulled it shut.

He didn't know why the sight of that man holding his wife and daughter's hand bothered him so. Larry had seen much worse not long ago—walked into the bedroom he shared with his wife to witness her sliding up and down that motherfucker's dick. Her back turned to him, Paul blindfolded on some kinky shit, neither of them saw Larry. He stood there, watching them make love. It both hurt and shocked Larry, even though he knew it shouldn't have, considering he had been the one to hire Paul, giving the man permission to keep Marian busy.

Considering all of that, why was Larry surprised to see what was before him now?

He pushed open the Corolla door and hurried up the street behind his family and the man trying to steal them away.

Larry ducked behind a tree when he thought Jabari was about to turn and glance over his shoulder. Peeking back out at the four of them, Larry was surprised even more when Jabari and Simone broke away from their mother and Paul, leaving the two adults strolling the path...still hand in hand, as though they were in love.

After seeing this, Larry was out from behind his cover, walking angrily down the path in their direction. He would confront them, find out exactly what the hell was going on. Find out why his wife would allow his children to see her behave that way with one man, when she would not even allow their own father to visit them.

Stomping furiously toward them, not ten feet behind, Larry stopped. Heart aching and pounding at the same time, he stood, ready to make a scene in font of his children and everyone—the joggers, bikers, the dog walkers—whoever wanted to witness him go crazy. But he knew that would accomplish nothing. He needed to exercise control, maybe go another route.

In the middle of the path, he turned, started back toward the Toyota, believing maybe it was time he paid Paul a visit.

11

Holding the phone, waiting for Paul to answer, Larry remembered watching him yesterday as he, Marian and the kids, loaded back into the Lexus after their walk through the park.

Larry followed them to a Brewster's ice cream shop, watched them sit around a table licking cones, and laughing, then head back to the mansion.

He pulled up where he had parked before, as the mansion security gates close behind the truck.

Glancing at the dash clock in the Toyota, Larry saw that it was approaching 9 P.M. He lowered the seatback, relaxed, telling himself he'd wait there for Paul to leave, then follow the man to his ratty, project apartment, and have a talk with him there.

9 P.M. turned to 12 A.M. then to 2:47 A.M., and wiping his tired eyes, Larry forced himself to accept the fact that Paul was not going home, at least not that night.

He grabbed his cell phone from the passenger seat, glanced at it, and thought briefly about calling the man. He decided against it, believing tomorrow would be a better time to speak to him.

Looking at the phone more closely las tnight, he was surprised to see that Shreeva hadn't called, nor texted him once, figuring she was still upset about him not going to get the marriage licenses with her.

She'd get over it, Larry thought, tossing the phone back to the seat, starting the engine, and glancing back at the house one last time to make sure Paul wasn't walking out, as he pulled away.

Still holding the phone, Paul finally picked up.

"Bishop, what do you want?"

"We need to meet," Larry said.

"For what?"

"I need to talk to you, face to face."

There was a pause on the other end of the phone—Larry figuring Paul was debating whether it was smart to see his old employer.

After another beat, Paul said, "Fine. Ten after twelve, tomorrow in front of the High museum."

"That's not good for me," Larry lied, wanting things on his terms.

"Then we ain't meeting. I work around the corner. That's my lunch break. Take it or leave it."

Holding the phone to his ear, Larry noticed the boy's mouth had gotten a lot smarter since the days he took orders from Larry.

"Okay, whatever," Larry said. "Tomorrow."

At ten minutes past twelve, Larry approached his old employee who wore a pastel green collard shirt, khaki pants and loafers.

Paul pulled the sunglasses from his face, and stood up off the railing he was leaning on when he caught sight of Larry.

"Bishop." Paul extended a hand.

Larry looked down at it, sniffed, then looked away, leaning on the railing Paul had been resting against.

"What the fuck are you doing with my family?" Larry said, getting straight to it.

"Excuse me."

"I followed you yesterday. Walking around Piedmont, eating fucking ice cream with my kids. You think you're their Daddy?"

"No, but I'm thinking they're gonna need one, since the one they had is no longer around."

Larry flinched with the thought of swinging on Paul that moment. Paul was a big dude, but Larry wasn't tiny, and he definitely wasn't a punk.

"Try it," Paul said, as though having read Larry's thoughts. He stiffened, seemingly preparing to defend himself, as men in slacks and shirts, women wearing skirts and pants suits walked past them.

"I got this work shit on," Paul warned. "But I'll come out of it and put you down, you try anything."

Larry's name and face had already been all over the TV, the last thing he needed was to end up on the evening news after being carted off to jail for rolling around on the sidewalk, kicking and punching another grown man.

"You went back to my house last night, and you didn't leave," Larry said, trying not to think about what might have happened during the time Paul was there. "Why?"

"You're stalking your wife now? That's some sick shit, Bishop."

"Answer the question. Why were you there all night?"

"I sleep there sometimes. She doesn't feel comfortable being there alone."

"Why?"

Paul looked at Larry as though he was stupid. "She doesn't want to take a chance in you coming over and trying to get physical with her in order to see the kids."

Larry assumed Marian hadn't told him about the last time he was there. "So that's the only reason you were there?"

"One of the reasons."

"The other being?"

"We're together now."

"My wife is dating her personal assistant. She giving you allowance?" Larry said, sarcastically.

"I'm no ones personal assistant anymore," Paul said, offended. "I quit. And she don't got to pay me. I'm fucking your wife for free."

Larry stepped up in Paul's face. Eye to eye, they stared at each other, six inches between them, as cars passed on the street and pedestrians marched by, chatting, and sipping the last of their lunchtime sodas.

"I think you need to be careful, son," Larry warned. "Messing with a man's family. You playing with my kid's heads, making them think you gonna to be there when you're not."

"If she says yes, I will," Paul said.

"Says yes to what?"

"I proposed." Paul seemed genuinely happy about it. "It's fast. We know it. But we plan to have a long engagement," he said, like this was information Larry wanted to hear. "She hasn't come out and said yes yet, but she's excited, and I know she's just waiting to clear up all this nonsense with you."

Larry felt dizzy with the thought that Marian was trying to replace him as her husband, but he was downright infuriated and enraged that she might be trying to swap this man as their children's father.

"You have any kids?" Larry asked, not knowing why he didn't know the answer to this question, considering how extensively he thought he checked this man out before hiring him.

"What?" Paul hesitated.

"You heard me. Do you have any children?"

"A daughter. She's older. I don't know her, or where she is. And I imagine if I did, she wouldn't care to see me." Paul said, seeming hurt by the fact.

"Would you want some man to start playing with her feelings?"

"She's grown. I have no say. She can do what she wants."

"But what if this man was trying to hurt her?"

"I'm not trying to hurt your kids, Bishop. I love—"

Before Paul could finish his sentence, Larry had him by the throat, forced him backward, the small of his back banging against the railing. Paul did not fight back, allowed himself to be held, Larry figuring because he knew he was wrong in what he was about to say.

"Speak those words to me about my children again," Larry hissed. "I'll kill you, or won't be afraid to die trying." He snatched his hand from Paul's throat, then turned and hurried angrily away.

12

Larry climbed out of his Bentley and started across the street toward Shreeva's condo building when he heard his name called. He continued walking, not recognizing the voice, and not wanting to deal with someone who had an opinion about the kind of man he was, wanting to take it up with him that moment.

"Bishop Lakes," the voice called again.

Larry heard two pairs of hard bottomed shoes quickly slapping the pavement. Turning, he saw a couple of middle-aged men in suits trotting across the street, one of them black, the other white.

"Bishop Lakes," the black man said, flashing a gold detective's shield. "Sorry sir, but we're going to need for you to come with us, please."

"What's this about?" Larry asked. He backed away, the white man reaching out for him, grabbing his wrist.

"Take your hands off of me!" Larry said, snatching away. "I haven't done anything."

"If that's the case, sir, you should have no problem coming downtown to speak with us," the white detective said. "We'll bring you back here when we're done."

Half an hour later, Larry sat in another interrogation room, in another metal chair, at another metal table. Thankfully, this time his wrists were not cuffed and his face had not been shattered.

He sat there alone. William Watts was not with him or on his way. Larry was told he hadn't been arrested, had just been brought in for questioning, so there was no need for him to call his lawyer.

Looking up, he heard the door opening.

A tall, graying white man wearing a dark suit, walked into the room and closed the door. He flashed a smile, which disappeared by the time the man reached the table and pulled out a chair.

He sat across from Larry, and set his hands in his lap beneath the table's surface.

"Bishop Lakes, I'm Captain Vernon, Atlanta Police Department. I'm sorry to have had you brought in this way. My detectives told me you were—"

"Why am I here?" Larry said, not needing apologies.

"Yes, there is the matter of that." Another quick smile, then Vernon peeled back
the cover of the manila file he had been holding—the one Larry just noticed. Vernon pulled out a picture, and with his pointer finger, stabbed the photo and spun it upside down so that Larry could view it the right way. "Recognize this young man?"

"Yes," Larry said. "He was a member of my boy's ministry. His name is Urail Parker."

"*Was*," Captain Vernon said. "His name *was* Urail Greene. He's dead."

Larry gasped, sincerely taken aback by the shocking news. Had the boy been released from the hospital without Larry knowing, only to later be hit by a car, struck by a bullet or die in some freak accident? "What happened to him?"

"He was severally beaten some weeks ago. So bad he slipped in a coma he never came out of. He died last night."

"I'm sorry to hear that," Larry said. "But why am I here?"

"Another young man, supposedly a friend of this guy," Vernon said, tapping the photo of Urail, "...keeps calling us. Even came into the department saying that you're the reason Urail is dead...that you beat him."

"I didn't touch that boy!"

"Okay," Vernon said, coolly leaning back in the chair. "Did you know the man that did beat him? The boy said that was a possibility as well."

Looking into the captain's eyes to see if he was actually serious about this, Larry shook his head. "I didn't do this, and I don't know who did." He rose from his chair, paced the room a moment, genuinely grief stricken by the news he had just received. "I knew those boys for years. I mentored them, raised them as if they were my own sons."

"I've heard a little bit about that on the news," Vernon said, as if accusing Larry of something.

"What did you say?" Larry recognized the accusatory tone in his words, a tone he had heard in the past. He stood, pointing a trembling finger at the detective. "I have never been charged in regard to anything relating to those boys!"

"I'm sorry, Bishop. You're right. Please forgive me," Vernon stood, gesturing for Larry to sit back at the table. "I can tell you're shaken hearing of Urail's death. I can tell he meant a lot to you."

"He did!"

"And I'm sorry for your loss. Please, please, have a seat."

Larry lowered himself back into the chair.

Vernon grabbed the picture off the table and placed it back in the folder and closed it. "I had you brought in because of what Mr. Robby Gentry, told us. So even though you said no, I have to ask again, make sure I heard you correctly. Did you have Urail beaten?"

"No," Larry said, his hands folded tightly on the table's top.

"Did you hire, or give the order to the man that did have him beaten?"

"No."

"Do you have any information that might lead us to who is responsible for Urail's death."

"No!" Larry said, feeling himself starting to come undone.

Another insincere smile from Vernon. "Then we're all done here. You're free to go. I'll have my men take you back to wherever you want to go."

"Fine," Larry said, quickly getting out of the chair, wanting to be out of the detective's sight as quickly as possible.

"I know you want justice done and for us to find who did this to that poor boy," Detective Vernon said, as Larry reached for the door. "So I just want you to know that we're going to continue investigating Robby Gentry's accusations, claiming you had some hand in this."

Larry stared silent at the man, for it seemed as though he had something more to say.

"And if I find proof of your involvement, Bishop, I'll be sending someone to snatch you right up and bring you back." Vernon smiled. "Have a good day."

13

His Bentley was badly parked, one of the front wheels up on the curb, the other three in the street. It was sometime after midnight, Larry having no business being where he was. Exactly where that was, he wasn't sure. Outside of it being a rough neighborhood, somewhere in the shadow of the Turner Field baseball stadium, Larry had no clue as to where he stopped his car.

This day had been filled with nothing but devastating news. The word that Marian was actually considering marrying Paul, then the fact that he was being looked at by the police for Urail's death was almost too much for Larry to bear.

Yes, he sanctioned the beating. It was him that put Tyrell Suggs up to it, twice. But the intent was never for the boy to die. Even though Urail was no longer the bright, witty boy he had been years ago, Larry did still love him, and the idea of him no longer being among the living was something he was having a hard time accepts as real.

"Van, I need to see you! I'm sure you've heard. You need to call me back," Larry said, leaving a voice message for Van over an hour ago. It was the only message Larry had left him, after four of his calls went unanswered to Van's cell phone.

He had no idea if Van had his phone with him, or more likely, the boy was looking down at the screen each time it rang, seeing that it was Larry and choosing not to answer.

Although Van did as Larry wanted and didn't show for the mediation, which gave Larry his temporary victory, thinking he'd only have to give the boy's three hundred thousand dollars instead of the three million Marian was extorting from him, it seemed Van must've had second thoughts, must've felt guilty betraying his friends like that, for since then, Larry could never reach the boy on the phone.

He was sure Van must've heard the news of Urail's death, and he wondered if he believed as Robby did? That Larry had something to do with Urail being dead.

Larry let the phone drop out of his hand and fall to the car's floor as he reached across to the passenger seat, groping for the fifth of whisky he had already consumed half of.

He was drunk, and the rundown clapboard houses lining the trash littered streets started to blur at the edges and spin a little. But Larry wasn't as far gone as he needed to be to forget about all the despair that plagued him.

His head rolling around on his seat's headrest, he felt eyes on him.

He turned, looking out the driver's side window to see a frail man with a sunken face, dressed in filthy clothing on the corner, staring at him.

Larry paid him no mind, setting his thoughts on what else could be done to ease his suffering. He lunged across the car seats, reaching for the glove box after the thought hit him. He grabbed the small zipper bag out of the compartment, not bothering to close the door back.

Momentarily elated that he had chosen to carry some of what Jayteesh gave him, he unzipped the bag to reveal the items: spoon, lighter, tourniquet, syringe and small chunk of heroin.

Larry glanced out the window again as he warmed the drgu in the spoon, seeing two more men looking in his direction from across the street.

Carefully, he set the spoon with it's contents on the arm rest of the Bentley, pulled the drug into the syringe, then held it in his teeth. His sleeve already rolled up, he deftly fastened the rubber band around his bicep just as Jayteesh had done that night in the bathroom stall. He slapped the vein south of his bicep until it inflated under the skin.

The needle tip to the vein, Larry looked up to see two of the men who had been staring at him from the corner, now looking down on him from just outside the Bentley's door. Another man, just as gaunt, sunken-eyed and zombie-looking, stared from the open passenger side window.

His head whirling frantically now, Larry sunk the tip of he needle into his vein, pushing the poison into his system. Immediately, as every time he did this drug, it sped through his blood, euphorically numbing his senses. His eyes rolled back, catching sight of the men reaching for the handle of the door, pulling it open, and laying their hands on him to snatch him from the car.

Larry blinked against his white surroundings, the bright lights stabbing his retinas like acid mist. A dark blot stood in the center of his field of vision. He blinked until the lines came into focus, and he saw Shreeva standing in front of him.

"Where...where am I?" Larry said, looking around, coming to the conclusion that he was in a hospital room. "What happened?"

Shreeva neared his bed. She was dressed nicely as always, like she was about to attend an exclusive social gathering, not like she had gotten an emergency phone call from a nurse, said that Bishop Larry Lakes was found lying beaten in the middle of the street, his wallet and shoes stolen, and a needle sticking out of his arm. Exactly what Shreeva said happened.

"I guess whoever robbed you wanted your Bentley more than your cell phone. They found my number under your in case of emergency contact."

Shreeva sat down on the edge of the hospital bed. Only then did Larry see the crumpled wad of tissue in her right fist, and realized how pink her eyes were from crying.

"What were you doing over there, Larry?"

He frowned, trying to remember how he had gotten here, and why. He shook his head on the white pillowcase. "Don't know. Urail...he's dead. I...that news just hit me harder than I expected and—"

"You wanted to go to the hood and commit suicide by shooting heroin on a street corner? Is that it? Goddammit Larry, what has gotten into you?"

"Didn't I just tell you that—"

"I know," Shreeva said, rising from the bedside. "I know, I know, I know! You lost everything, you have nothing, no family, no church, you ain't got shit no more," Shreeva said, lowering her voice, as someone passed by the open door. "And I'm sorry that you're hurting. I told you that already a million times. I really am, but you're not the only one suffering. You do this shit to yourself, I feel it, too," Shreeva said, dabbing at fresh tears. "When did you start shooting dope?"

His eyes closed, Larry turned away ashamed. "Trying to deal with all this...not long ago."

"Good. Should make it fairly easy to quit then," Shreeva said. She closed the space between them, took Larry's hand and squeezed it. She paused a moment, as if having to force herself to speak the words. "What you're doing is self-destructive, and I'd be a fool to stand beside you when you explode." Shreeva lowered her face to Larry's hand, kissed it, "Get a handle on this Larry, soon."

14

Paul stood in the large room at the Atlanta Rehabilitation Center. It resembled his old high school gymnasium, hardwood floors, metal grates over the windows—everything but the basketball goals on either end of the room.

He hung out by the folding tables, stacked with plates of donuts, and a bowl of red punch beside two short columns of Styrofoam cups. He held one of the cups in his hand as he stared at the brown skinned woman, wearing cut off jean shorts and sandals. Her hair flowed to her shoulders, a diamond stud sparkled in her left nostril. The girl was chatting it up with some derelict types. A couple of white guys stood around her, tattoos crawling up out the necks of their t-shirts.

The girl glimpsed Paul, held his stare for a moment while she laughed at whatever was said to her by one of the men standing in front of her.

Losing his patience, Paul raised his wrist, pointed to his watch, conveying the need to speak to the girl that moment.

The young woman took hugs from the two men, then walked through the twenty or so folding chairs sitting in relatively straight aisles in the center of the big room.

She stopped in front of Paul, her arms crossed, looking as though she had better things to do. "What is it, Paul?"

"I told you don't call me that, Shayla. It's Dad, or nothing at all."

"Then it's nothing at all. What is it?"

Paul shook his head at the girl's attitude, but he knew she had a right to it. She was nineteen years old, and before Paul set out on the lengthy task of hunting her down, the last time he had seen his daughter was when he had made a brief appearance at her fifth birthday party, dropping off an unwrapped doll he picked up at the dollar store.

Shayla's mother, the girl Paul accidently got pregnant, Crysta was sixteen when she told him she was having the baby, and expected him to participate in the raising of the child, as much as he did in the kid's conception.

Paul was not interested in playing the father when he was still a boy himself. He wasn't there for Shayla's birth, or many of the other milestones he should've been present for. But over the course of the next five years, he contributed a few bucks here and there for diapers, formula, and clothes. It wasn't enough, Crysta always said whenever Paul came by her apartment to have sex with the girl, which was only when he knew Crysta's mother wasn't home.

He only saw his daughter because it was a condition for getting in Crysta's panties. She would make him hold Shayla, make him feed her a bottle, rock her to sleep and promise that he would take her to the park, or play with her down on the apartment floor, before Crysta even thought about reaching behind her back and unsnapping her bra, or pushing down her pants.

As time passed, Paul saw Crysta less frequently. There were other men, and Paul tried to play the jealous father. But Crysta would call him on his behavior, tell him she was only dating this guy or that guy because he wasn't around, then tell him how ridiculous he sounded acting as though he cared anything about his daughter when she knew he didn't and never had.

Paul told Crysta she was wrong about him. She told Paul to prove it.

His appearance at the child's birthday was his very weak attempt at showing Crysta what kind of father he was. Paul did exactly that, by not staying even fifteen minutes. He walked into the kitchen where the half-dozen kids played, saw Shayla sitting at the table, a party hat strapped to her head, big ponytails of thick hair hanging over he ears. Paul scooped his little girl up, held her in his arms, wished her a happy birthday and kissed her on the cheek. He apologized, and told her he had to go.

"Where are you going, Daddy?"

Caught off guard, he stammered, trying to think of an answer, and was only able to come up with, "To the store. But…I'll be right back."

Her bottom lip poked out, eyes sad, she wrapped her tiny arms around his neck, as though she'd never see him again. She would've been right, if at age 36 Paul hadn't started feeling guilty about the little girl he had abandoned.

Over the years, there was always some intention Paul hadn't acted on to try to find his daughter. But he never really took it seriously until he got the job as Marian Lakes's personal assistant. He saw how much Bishop's children idolized him, wanted to spend every waking moment with their father, and how disappointed they were—especially little Simone—by how often he wasn't there.

Paul decided to find his little girl, started doing a simple Google search of Shayla's mother's name. After two weeks of internet searches, calls made and visits to government records offices, he found out that Crysta died not even a year ago from a drug overdose. He was able to come up with an address, and asked some of the neighbors when they last saw Shayla, Crysta's daughter. A woman told Paul that she had seen Shayla hanging around at the rehab center.

Two days later, Paul saw his daughter hanging outside of the building, smoking cigarettes with a small group of people.

Staring out at her from the driver's seat of the Lincoln Town Car, Paul felt ashamed, like he had no business even going over there claiming to be her father. He knew if he did, she'd probably curse him out, spit in his face, tell him she never wanted to see him again. He climbed out of the car, approached her, and that was exactly what Shayla did and said.

But Paul vowed to return, to win his daughter back, and make up for the fact that she was experiencing the hard times she was going through.

So for the last six months, Paul had been visiting Shayla a few times a week, every now and again attending one of her meetings, but most times just hanging out talking, trying to get to know her all over again.

"What do you want?" Shalya asked, the first time he visited her at the rehab center. She looked him up and down like the very sight of him sickened her.

He asked to be allowed a visit with her a few times a week, saying all he wanted to do was talk. Paul told her he wouldn't try to play the father, wouldn't try to assert any fatherly authority on her, because he knew he had lost that right.

"Half an hour, just you and me, a few times a week. That's all," he had asked.

Shayla gave him that, and for those first thirty days, she sat outside with her father, her back to him, or she'd look off in the distance, or wear her earbuds and bob her head to whatever was playing on her iPod. After not having said a word to him for that period, but having met her obligation of thirty minutes in his presence, she'd get up and go back into the rehab center.

But Paul stuck it out as he said he would, and now they were here.

It wasn't quite the perfect family relationship, but at least his daughter was talking to him.

"How was the meeting today?" Paul asked, most of the attendees starting to leave after they had partaken of the free after-meeting refreshments.

"It was cool," Shayla said.

"Good." Paul set down his punch on the table. "Can your father get a hug?"

Shayla gave him a look suggesting she questioned his sanity. It was the same look she gave him over the last few months he had been asking. He was not surprised to see the scrunched up nose and pursed lips, but was shocked when she nodded, opened her arms a little, huffed and said, "Yeah, I guess."

Paul took Shayla in his arms, realizing it had been almost fifteen years since he had held her. He closed his eyes, squeezed her tight and would've gotten emotional, hadn't Shayla said, "Okay, okay. You're gonna break my ribs already."

"Sorry," Paul said, backing away. "Can we talk a minute? You wanna step outside with me? I got a little news I want to share with you."

Shayla huffed again, as though anything dealing with her father was an inconvenience. "Fine, okay."

Outside, Shayla stood leaning against the side of the building, Paul standing in front of her.

"You been all right?" Paul asked.

"Been fine," Shayla said.

Not knowing what else to say, Paul dug in his wallet, pulled out six twenties, folded them and held them out to his daughter. "Take it."

"Put your money away, Dad. You can't buy me."

"I'm not trying to. Just take the money. Unless you don't need it."

Shayla stared at Paul, shook her head, then took the folded bills and stuffed it in the back pocket of her jean short. "Thanks," she said under her breath.

"Program going okay? You ain't been using, have you?"

"What?" Her voice high pitched, Shayla sounded as though she didn't appreciate the question.

"Don't what me," Paul said. "I asked you a question. And be honest."

"No. I haven't been using, but it's only because I can't get any."

"You don't mean that."

"You said be honest," Shayla said. "They say the urge passes as the program continues, but I'm telling you, if I had some drugs, I'd use the shit out of them."

"You better be joking," Paul said, wondering what, if anything he could do to stop his daughter from falling back down that hole.

"The conversation is riveting, but I'm not gonna stay out here with you all day. You said you got news. What is it?"

Paul battled with whether to tell Shayla about the engagement, but finally decided it was the right thing to do. With this second chance he had gotten with his daughter, he wanted everything to be out in the open.

"The lady I told you I used to work for as a personal assistant...we're engaged." Paul held his breath, waited for the reaction.

Shayla looked sad, Paul figuring she was probably thinking about her mother, wondering why he never married her.

"Good for you," Shayla said.

"I know things didn't work out the way you wanted between me and your—"

"No," Shayla said. "I'm not a child, Dad. Life is complicated. It's not a fairytale. Most of it's bullshit, so if anyone is lucky enough to get something good out of it, I say good for them." She smiled a little. "So I meant it when I said I was happy for you."

Relieved, Paul grabbed his daughter in a hug. It was a quick one. He released her, stepped back and said, "I didn't wanna break your ribs so..."

"Naw," Shayla smiled. "This time its all right."

15

"Pull over right here," Larry said to Tyrell Suggs.

After Shreeva warned him at his hospital bed that she could only tolerate so much more ridiculous behavior from him, Larry reached out a hand for her. She looked reluctantly over at him.

"Please, just let me say something," Larry said.

She came to him as he knew she would, taking his hand and setting again beside him on the bed.

"You're right. What's done is done," Larry said. "I can't continue to let it mess up all the good I still have, namely you. You won't ever have to go through any of this nonsense again. I promise."

Shreeva stared down at Larry as though she truly wanted to believe him, but was having a hard time. "And the nights you come in late, sometimes not at all? Larry, that has to stop. I don't know where you are, and..."

"It's over. Done," Larry said. "You still my fiancé?" He managed a smile despite the pain he felt from the facial injuries he sustained during the beating he had taken on the street.

Shreeva smiled back, but shook her head at the same time. "If some craziness like this happens again, I'm telling you—"

"I know, I know," Larry said. "You're gone. I understand."

Tyrell Suggs pulled his Monte Carlo alongside the curb of a large Baptist church, Tyrell Suggs chauffeuring Larry around in his car, since the Bentley was gone. It had been stolen while Larry lay out cold on the street, hopped up on heroin. Larry figured it was probably already chopped up and dismantled in some garage an hour outside of Atlanta. Didn't make him any difference. The car wasn't his much longer anyway.

Larry stood up out of the car, gazed up at the church he had never been in, but passed on a few occasions over the years. He leaned back down and into the passenger window of Tyrell Suggs's car.

"I just want to step in here a second. I need a moment to sort some things out."

Tyrell Suggs nodded, reclined some in his seat, as if knowing he would be there a while.

"Take your time, Bishop. Do what you have to do."

After stepping gingerly up the walkway—his leg must've been injured somehow while he was being beaten—Larry stopped at the wooden church double doors. He grabbed one of the handles, prayed that the church was open, and gave it a pull.

The door opened and inside the space was lit with low, dim lights. He stepped straight into the sanctuary. The ceiling was high, stain glass windows were everywhere, and the faint odor of must and old wood permeated the interior of the structure.

Larry walked slowly up the aisle, soiled, tread-bare carpet beneath him, old wooden pews stretching out to the far ends of the sanctuary. He imagined them on Sunday mornings filled with worshiping parishioners, their hands raised, crying, screaming, stomping their feet, taken over by the spirit—giving it up for Jesus!

It was what he would miss most about having his church, Larry thought as he halted in front of the alter, looking up to the enormous cross suspended high above him. He would miss his people, his congregation, those that loved him, trusted and depended on him to give them the word of God each week. That had been taken from him, and as Larry settled down to his knees, he still battled with accepting that this was his fate. After all he had been through, after all that he had sacrificed to do God's biding, he asked himself why he was being punished the this way.

"Why?" He said aloud, his voice low, reverent…at first. "Why would you do this to me?"

His head lowered, palms together, eyes closed, his fingertips pressed lightly against his lips, he tried to quiet himself, wait for the answer that God would deliver him. He heard nothing, the silence panicking him. Had he lost his connection to God? Was he no longer blessed or worthy enough to have His ear? Or was He angry with Larry?

"Don't…don't, please," Larry mumbled, bending forward, his back curved over his thighs, rocking. "Don't leave me. Tell me that you won't leave me." Again he listened, waited for a sign of any sort, but he saw nothing, heard nothing. He raised his head, eyes opening slowly, his lower lids shiny with tears balanced there, having yet to fall. He peered up at the cross.

"Why are you doing this to me? Am I not human? Am I not fallible? Can I not be forgiven?" His voice echoed against the high vaulted ceilings. "All that I've done for you!" He pulled himself to his feet, pointed a finger to the cross. "The way I loved you, you cannot forgive me for being what you fucking created!"

No answer. Still silence, save for the faint sound of shuffling, coming from some distant room in the bowels of the church.

"Answer me," Larry stomped a foot. "Answer me, motherfucker!" He yelled, spun, raised both his fists in the air, as if wanting God to ascend from the heavens so they could handle their business there on earth, in the middle of the tiny church, like men.

"Sir."

Larry whirled around, startled to see a man, older, possibly twenty years Larry's senior, standing just outside of an open door Larry hadn't noticed. He wore glasses, a dark suit. He looked frail, held a hand against the doorframe as though for support.

"Sir, you have to go," he told Larry. Although phrased as an order, it was more a passive request.

"Who are you?"

"Deacon Marshall. I'm sorry, but you have to leave. We can't allow that kind of behavior—"

"I'm grieving," Larry said, taking a single step toward the man. "I've come here to lay my burdens down at God's feet, pray that He help me, and you tell me I have to leave."

"Sir, I heard what you were saying. How you used the Lord's name in vain, and—"

"Do you know who I am?" Larry said. Two more steps he took toward the man. Deacon Marshall shuffled back just a bit.

"I don't."

"I had a church several times this size. There was no one we would not help, no one we would turn away. Didn't matter what their ailments, their issues, their transgressions were, they could all be repaired, all be forgiven with God's help. That's what I was taught," Larry said, watching as the man dragged another foot back, as if to retreat into the door he emerged from. "That's what I taught in my church. Yet, in my time of need, you tell me I must leave?"

Larry didn't know what spooked the man, what had his eyes widen behind his little metal eye glass frames. Was it the high pitch anger in Larry's voice, or the fists clenched by his sides, or the look of rage that Larry felt covering his face? Whatever it was, Deacon Marshall must've gotten in his head that he was in danger, turned, and hobbled as quickly as his aging body would allow, back into the room. It wasn't quick enough.

Behind him, Larry slapped his hands on the old man's back before he was two feet inside small office. He spun the man around, threw him to a wall, then grabbed him by the front of his suit jacket, snatching them face to face.

"I ask you a question and you run from me?" Larry said, breathing heavy in Marshall's face.

"I'm sorry," the deacon said, trembling.

"Is that why I can't hear Him in this place?"

"What?" Marshall asked, his voice broken by fear.

"There's a cross in that room, yet God is not in this house!" Larry shook Marshall violently. "I cannot speak to Him. I cannot hear Him, so I'll speak to you."

"Sir, please, if you just leave," Marshall mumbled, his glasses askew, his eyes shut tight.

"Why did He take my church?" Larry asked, seeing the memory of himself forced to sign his precious building over to Bonner.

"Sir, I don't know who you're talking about."

"My family, my children!" Larry's mind flooded with the images of Paul walking hand-in-hand with Marian, with his children—his wife in a wedding dress, sharing a kiss with that man. "He's taken my wife from me!" Larry yelled, throwing Marshall against the wall again.

70

The old man banged the back of his skull, cried a high-pitched scream

"Tell me why!" Larry said, then saw Marshall double over after not answering fast enough. Larry hadn't realized it until he looked down, saw the fist he held, the fist that had struck Marshall in the gut. "Why won't you answer me?"

"Please," Marshall cried from one knee, his head lowered, a trembling palm held over his head, gesturing for Larry to stop.

But there was no stopping. No stopping when Larry was a young man, bent over in the back seat of a car, his face stuffed into it's cushions, some grown man relentlessly raping him, as though Larry was his property. There was no stopping when he lay homeless on a curb, his stomach turning in on itself from hunger. No stopping when all that he loved, all that he worked for, all that he believed himself to be was snatched from him. All of those thoughts banged around in Larry's head as he stood outside himself, watched as he kicked, beat and stomped Deacon Marshall to the floor. Rage-filled, crying and yelling, Larry smashed the man's hands with his shoes, kicked him in the ribs, pummeled him till Marshall lay bleeding, writhing, one of his legs twitching like an animal needing to be put down.

Standing over him, Larry heard the old man whispering something. He bent down to hear him.

"Please...please...help...God!"

Larry stood, raised the heel of his shoe. "God can't hear you anymore, just like he can't hear me," Larry said, then kicked the man in the face.

Outside, Larry climbed into the passenger seat of Tyrell Suggs's Monte Carlo. He slammed the door, wiped the last of the sweat from his skull with his handkerchief, then calmly slipped the rag back into his suit jacket pocket.

"Everything cool, Bishop?" Tyrell Suggs asked, sitting up in his seat and starting the car.

Staring out the window, Larry nodded his head. "Yeah, everything is fine."

16

Things were quickly coming undone.

After Tyrell Suggs pulled up to his house, he started to exit the car, but stopped.

"You okay, Bishop?" Tyrell Suggs asked, when he noticed Larry hadn't moved, just continued starting out the car's windshield, his hands folded in his lap.

"I'm fine," Larry said, his eyes still forward. "I'm gonna need your other car again to get around if you don't mind." He turned to look at his friend.

"Its all yours. You know you don't need to ask."

Larry was appreciative. It was what he needed, someone that was still devoted to him, unlike his wife, unable to stand by him when he needed her most. Unlike his children, who seemingly accepted the fact that they'd have a new father—even though they had little control over the situation Marian constructed there at the house—they could've protested when they were given this news.

Couldn't they see Paul was trying to take his place? They could, Larry assured himself, and had to control his anger thinking that both Jabari and Simone—especially the boy, being older and knowing better—should've been punished in some way.

"Bonner planting those drugs, taking the church still messing with you, Bishop?" Tyrell Suggs asked.

Still lost in his thoughts, his eyes glazed over, looking at nothing but his anger, Larry nodded. "Mmm, hmm."

"I know you said you ain't wanna do nothing to the man—retaliate in any way for the foulness of what he did, but I think he got a lesson to learn."

Larry sat quietly listening to the drone of Tyrell Suggs deep, scratchy voice.

"I'm still willing to do whatever you want to give him what he got coming," Tyrell Suggs said. "I know you said you don't want to, but—"

"Tell me what you have in mind," Larry said.

Later, Larry had driven the old Toyota over to the run down neighborhood in Southeast Atlanta where Van lived. Before he had driven over there, sitting in the car, the manual window cranked halfway down, Larry called the boy several times—every single one of the calls going unanswered. He left three messages, saying pretty much the same thing. He needed to see Van. He really needed to see him.

Larry knew he was indeed losing it. That shit that happened in the church earlier was uncalled for, he knew, even though he wasn't fully aware of just what exactly happened.

A mental breakdown?

Much of it he didn't even remember. He was only able to hold on to bits—the smell of the old the church, Deacon Marshall's screams as Larry continuously kicked him. His eyes staring big, glossy and wet up at Larry, it looked as though the old man was sure he'd die.

As though he wasn't already in enough trouble—the police pulling Larry in for questioning, trying to pin Urail's death on him—all he needed was to be charged for half beating an old man to death. Thankfully, Larry remembered the deacon saying he had no idea who he was.

With all that mess in his head, Larry told himself he needed to see Van, just needed to be held, be told that he was loved, that everything was going to be fine. And he needed to release some of the horrible tension that was building in him; the stress he knew caused him to explode all over that man. If he didn't get this stuff out of him soon, there was no telling what else he would do.

Half an hour later, Larry knocked on Van's door, simultaneously thumbing his cell to ring Van's phone. No answer at the door, but from behind it, Larry heard a phone ringing and another noise—something accidently dropping to the floor—then the ringing abruptly stopped.

The boy was in there. Larry banged again, this time with enough force to rattle the entire frame.

"I'm not leaving till you tell me why you're avoiding me. Open the damn door, Van!"

The door opened, but was stopped by the security chain. Van stared out at Larry through the narrow space.

"What is this, Van? Open the door."

"I don't wanna talk to you. I don't need to talk to you ever again."

Van moved to shut the door. Larry shoved his foot in the space, stopping it.

"Open this damn door. Let me in so we can talk, or I swear I'll break this thing down."

Van stared through the crack in the door, as if to gauge just how serious the threat.

Larry narrowed his eyes, letting him know it was damn serious.

"Fine," Van relented.

Larry stepped back, let Van close the door and lower the chain.

He walked into the tiny apartment, turning to see Van still holding the door, as if afraid what might happen once it was closed.

"Shut the door, Van," Larry said.

Van closed the door.

He grabbed Van by the shoulders and pulled him in to kiss him. Van shook himself free, stumbled backward, appearing disgusted.

"What is your problem?" Larry said. "You ignore my calls, won't call me back and now I can't touch you?"

"You killed him, didn't you?" Van said. "You had Urail beaten, and now he's dead."

"Who told you that? Robby?"

"You did it so that he couldn't be at the mediation, so you wouldn't have to pay as much money."

"No," Larry lied. "You're wrong. Robby's wrong. None of that makes sense, and none of it is important. All that matters now is you being here for me—us being here for each other. I need you, Van." He brushed his trousers with his hand, drawing Van's attention to the noticeable bulge his hardened penis cast.

Van shook his head. "No, no, I'm done."

The words shocked Larry. After all he had given that boy, he never thought Van would turn on him.

"What? Exactly what do you think you're done with?"

"This," Van said. "You and me. You're not the man you say you are, but the man that everyone else accuses you of being. I don't wanna see you anymore. We're done. Get out!" He pointed toward the door.

When Larry didn't budge, Van started toward the door, as if to open it and wait while Larry slowly walked out, his head lowered in shame.

"You don't fucking decide when you're done with me," Larry said, raising his voice. "After all I've given you, all I've done for you! Get the fuck over here!" He reached out, grabbed Van by an arm. With the other hand, he grabbed Van by the face, held him tight, pressed his lips to his, kissing him as the boy fought to free himself.

"Don't! Don't, Bishop!" Van cried.

Larry didn't hear a word. He didn't hear the cries, the breathless gasps as Van struggled to free himself from Larry's hold. He spun Van around, threw him against the small kitchenette table, reached around the boy, angrily fumbling with his belt.

"No! Stop!" Van cried, louder.

"Shut up!" Larry demanded, snatching his jeans down, his underwear with them to expose his bare behind.

Larry yanked down his own pants, his penis stiff. He kicked Van's feet apart, opening his legs, preparing him for Larry to take.

"Please! Pleeeeeeaaaaassse, no!" Van screamed as though Larry was already in him, ripping his insides up, which was what Larry intended, take out every bit of frustration he had on the boy.

Larry stuffed his fingers in his mouth, coating them with spit. He lubricated his penis, then grabbed it, throbbing and threatening to explode the moment it was inserted.

Continuing to struggle and cry, Van swatted the table, pushing the dishes and glasses to the floor where they shattered. "I'm sorry!" Van screamed. "I'm sorry! Please don't! I'm so sorry."

All of a sudden, Larry froze. Van's last words, echoing in Larry's head, chilling his skin and sinking deep into his core. He was transported back to when he screamed the exact same words, to when he was held down, face smashed against the table, his father's hand pressed to the back of his head.

Lincoln used to take what he wanted when Larry would not willingly give it to him. Then Larry, in pain, screaming, crying, after begging not to be taken, after praying to God to spare him, would resort to apologizing to his father. Larry had done nothing wrong, in no way deserved to be molested by the man that was supposed to love him more than life, but Larry screamed his apologies anyway, taking responsibility for whatever wretched acts committed against the man that would make him want to do that to his own son.

Laying there, the man inside of him, grunting, sweating, cursing with the energy it took to chop wood or dig a ditch, Larry told himself he would never ever do such a horrible thing to anyone in his life.

Now, his hand still on Van's body—jettisoned back to the present, back to Van's apartment, the boy still apologizing to Larry—he looked down, his dick still in one of his fists, he saw that he was no longer erect. He took his hand from Van's hip, stepped back from him, dazed, as if not knowing what he was about to do and why.

Van turned, looked over his shoulder, then flipped around, yanked his pants back up, brushed against the table, fell to the floor, then scurried backward against a wall, crablike, on his hands and feet. "Get out!" Van yelled.

Larry slowly bent down, pulled his own pants up, shaking his head, taking backward steps. "I'm...I'm sorry, Van."

"Get the fuck out!" Van cried, smearing tears from his face. "Come here again, I'll call the police!"

"Okay, okay," Larry heard himself say, reaching behind himself for the door, pulling it open, then stepping out.

17

The next day, Larry stepped into a Buckhead Starbucks coffee, scanned the room, looking for his wife.

Yesterday, after losing his mind with Van, then actually losing Van, Larry sat parked out front of Shreeva's condo building, the phone pressed to his ear, praying that Marian picked up. She had every right not to, but he was still the father of their children, still her husband, the man she had loved for so many years, the man she had sworn, under God, to respect all of her life.

"Larry, why are you calling me?" Marian asked, finally picking up.

"To apologize for the last time I saw you. I had no right putting my hands on you."

"Fine. Goodbye."

"Wait, wait, wait! I need to see you."

"No! Not after what you—"

"Marian, I know the way things are now between us. I've accepted that," he lied. "Just let me talk to you, and I promise, you will never have to hear from me again."

He spotted Marian in a corner table of the crowded restaurant. She had agreed to meet him, but only in public.

"Hello, Marian," Larry said, standing in front of the table a moment before pulling his chair to sit. The pause was to see if she would stand, allow him to hug her, give her a kiss on the cheek. None of that was made available to him.

Larry sat. "Would you like something to drink? Some coffee?"

"If I did, I would buy it myself. Besides, you need to be saving your money to pay those boys."

Forcing a smile, Larry said, "They'll be taken care of."

"Why am I here?"

He knew he told his wife that he accepted the situation, but couldn't help admitting, "I miss you."

Marian shouldered her bag, scooted her chair back and prepared to stand. Larry quickly reached for her hand.

"Don't touch me!" she said loud enough to draw the attention of coffee sippers and raise heads that had been lowered behind laptop computer screens.

"I'm sorry, but please, please," Larry said, taking his hand back, lowering them both to his knees, below the surface of the table. "Just sit back down. I won't mention us again."

Marian stared skeptically at her husband, then sat back down.

"How are my children?"

"They're fine."

"Do they miss me?"

"I don't know," Marian said, uncomfortably shifting in her chair, looking away, her arms crossed over her chest. "I imagine they probably do."

"Even with Paul taking my place, playing father?"

Marian looked surprised and a little guilty.

"I've spoken to him. You should've told me that you plan to marry him."

She appeared ashamed that the news had gotten out. "I never said that. He asked me, but I never said for sure I'd go through with it."

"Will you?"

"I don't know if that's any of your business."

"He'll be living under the same roof as my children," Larry said, leaning forward over the table, lowering his voice when he said, "You goddamn right that's business of mine."

"Whether it is or not, you have no power, no control, no say any longer as to what happens with Jabari and Simone. But if you must know," Marian said, leaning back in her chair some. "I think I will marry him."

The way she said it, like throwing knives at him, Larry questioned if she was telling the truth, or just trying to hurt him. "You can't do that."

"I can and you can't stop me."

"You won't."

"Fucking try me, Larry."

He exhaled, slumping some in the chair. He shook his head, closed his eyes, folded his arms, and wished he could just retreat, go somewhere and wake up to find that all of this was just a bad nightmare.

"What is it?" Marian asked, sounding like she hated the fact she still cared something about him, but needed to know, at least that he wasn't about to leap from a building and kill himself. He was still the father of her children.

Clinching his teeth, pressing his arms hard against his ribs, Larry opened his eyes, knowing the tears he was holding back would fall. They did, and he hated that he allowed his wife to see him like that.

"You can't do this to me. Take my children, marry another man, leave me penniless."

"Larry—" Marian started.

"If you knew what I've been going through, what I've done."

"What did you do?" she asked, urgency in her voice.

"Nothing," he lied. "Why would you marry him? You don't love him."

"You don't know that."

"Do you?"

Again Marian appeared uncomfortable, rubbing her arms, averting her eyes. "It doesn't matter if I love him or not. There are other reasons, too."

"What other reasons?" Larry said, preparing to brace against yet more pain.

"You don't want to know."

"Tell me."

Marian stared unblinking into Larry's eyes. Her mind was working, calculating the good against the bad of disclosing whatever it was she had to say. He'd seen her do this over the years they were married, often times coming out of her mouth with some bombshell of an admission.

"Just tell me, Marian!" Larry ordered, trying not to sound too forceful.

"Jabari needs a father figure since you'll no longer be in his life."

Shocked, Larry felt his entire body go numb.

"What did you just—"

"Jabari likes Paul. Both the kids do, and—"

"Shut up!" Larry whispered harshly, slapping a hand on the table. "You can't trust that man with my son. To do everything a real father...everything that I would—"

"I can, Larry."

"What makes you think—"

"Because he loves Jabari. He loves Simone, and he loves me," Marian said, standing from the table, lifting her purse up onto her shoulder. "And to answer the question you asked me earlier, the answer is yes. I love him, too."

"Don't do this, Marian," Larry said, standing, watching as his wife walked away from him. "Marian!" He yelled, feeling the eyes of those sitting around him. "Marian, don't you fucking do this, or I swear you'll be sorry!"

She didn't turn to acknowledge his threat, didn't even slow her stride, but sped up, hurrying out the store, down the sidewalk, then out of sight.

18

Not two hours later, Larry stood in the doorway of his father's nursing home room, the smell of Lysol and mildewed clothes assaulting his nose. The TV was on. An old, nineteen-inch set sat on a desk. His father Lincoln dozed in a vinyl covered easy chair, his head titled to one side.

Larry stood there in the doorway, just gazing at the man, as he had been doing for the last couple of minutes.

Lincoln raised his hand to scratch his face, opened an eye, then jumped, startled, grabbing tight to the arms of his chair when he saw that he was being watched. "What are you doing there just looking at me?"

"Been thinking about you, Dad," Larry said, taking a step into the room. "Lot's going in my life."

"Is your family okay? My grandchildren?"

Larry thought it funny how his father claimed possession of the children he had never seen. Because of all the horrible things Lincoln had done to Larry as a child and as a teen, Larry decided the man would never his see his grandchildren, let alone be left with them alone.

"Everybody is fine, Dad," Larry lied, determining it would make no sense to tell him the truth.

"And the business with the church. The boys didn't—"

"Like I said, everything worked out fine. The lawsuit...I won. I'm still preaching."

"But I saw on the news that your church has a new pastor, and—"

"It's temporary," Larry said, looking around the small room. He sat on the edge of his father's bed, facing Lincoln, Marian's face still in his head—

that awful way she looked at him when he tried to touch her—like he was some kind of pervert, some monster that wanted to hurt her and their children.

But despite how much Larry tried to deny that, tried to rationalize himself into being something other than that—anything other than that—wasn't that what he truly was?

The discs Marian found proved that, or she wouldn't have asked for the divorce. She wouldn't be demanding that he give those boys every fucking cent he had to his name, and she wouldn't have been attempting to get full custody of Larry's children. If he weren't the creature Marian saw every time she looked at him, Larry wouldn't be going through the hell he was experiencing that moment.

"What's wrong with you, boy?" Lincoln asked.

Larry blinked his father into focus. He had been staring in his direction, but was deep in thought. "What?"

"Why you looking at me like that?"

"I'm sorry," Larry said, attempting to shake the thoughts out of his head. "I was just thinking, is all."

"About what? Everything's not all right like you said, is it?"

Lincoln's physical health was fading; he was becoming old and frail. But mentally, the old man was still there.

"Everything is fine," Larry continued to lie. He hated him, and he wondered if Lincoln could see the loathing he felt for him in Larry's eyes. Larry attributed all the pain, all the heartache he felt and that which he caused, to his father. He figured it was the reason he drove all the way over here—to confirm that suspicion. It definitely wasn't to see how the man was doing, because Larry didn't give a damn.

If he had received the call saying that his father had passed in the night, and had been asked when he was coming to retrieve the body, Larry would've told them never. "Do with him what you want. Bury, burn him, or set him out in the alley with the rest of the trash. I don't care." That's what he would've said.

He stood from the bed, still staring at Lincoln.

"Where you going?" Lincoln asked.

"Leaving," Larry said, not feeling the need to waste anymore words on the man.

"You came all the way over here just to sit a minute, then leave?"

I can't stand the sight, the smell or the thought of you anymore, Larry wanted to say, but instead said, "Just thought I'd say hi."

"Okay," Lincoln said. He opened his arms. They shook as he strained to reach toward Larry. "Then give me a hug."

Larry froze, remembering how frightened he would be when his father would ask him for a "hug" when Larry was a child. He felt a bit of that fear even now, but had to remind himself that he no longer had to. His father had scarred him, transformed him into the beast he was, but Larry no longer had to cower in the man's presence or submit to him when he asked.

"I have to go, Dad," Larry said, walking toward the door. But before walking out, he stopped, turned back, not knowing why, but needing to ask the question. "You do know what you did to me, don't you, Dad?"

Lincoln looked surprised by the question. "What are you talking about?"

"All those years…the abuse. You damaged me."

"But…I apologized," Lincoln said, his eyes and the words filled with both guilt and regret.

"I know," Larry said, feeling himself smiling a little as though not to make his father feel too bad. "But an apology can't wash all you did to me away. I just need to know that you realize that. Do you?"

Lincoln sorrowfully lowered his head and nodded. "I do, son. I do."

19

Tyrell Suggs waited, parked by the curb, outside of the wide, gray, nondescript one story building. He had seen this place before, been inside for reasons he would like to forget.

On a small plaque bolted to the building, just beside the double glass entry doors, read Atlanta Drug Rehabilitation Center.

Inside, on any given weekday, chairs were lined up in a room the size of a small gymnasium, a podium set out in front where some haggard old woman, beaten up by the streets, stood and lectured an audience—people who may have experienced similar things, had been strung out and abused by a drug addiction they could not control. It didn't matter what kind: weed, heroin, coke, crack, whatever the fuck. They were all junkies, all did some wrong, most likely motivated by the drug that landed them in a police cell, or homeless on the street. This spot was a way to try to shake the habit, get clean and hopefully start a new life. It had worked for Tyrell Suggs many years ago, but he wondered just why had Paul, the guy who used to be Mrs. Lakes's assistant, walked into that spot an hour ago.

Last night, Bishop called Tyrell Suggs sounding pretty down.

"Can you do something for me?" he asked.

"Name it."

"I spoke to my wife earlier today. She plans to marry that bastard, Paul, and expects him to be father to my children, as she revokes my legal right to see them."

"I'm sorry, Bishop. That shit ain't no way right."

"I spoke to him, asked him if he had kids, asked him how he'd like it if someone played with his children like that."

"And?"

"He said he has a daughter, but hasn't seen or spoken to her in years."

"And you wanna know if he's telling the truth about that," Tyrell Suggs said.

"Yeah."

"I'll follow him around, see what I can see."

Pursuit started this morning, tailing Paul's Dodge Charger from the Lakes's mansion into midtown where the man pulled into a parking structure. Tyrell Suggs followed the car in, pulling a ticket from the machine, waiting for the gate to rise, then parked across the aisle, so that he'd be facing his car whenever Paul left.

After a full work day, eight hours, Paul was on the road again, Tyrell Suggs following behind him, but not so close as to be made.

Tyrell Suggs watched as the Dodge circled around the drive-thru at McDonald's then followed the car till it pulled up into the parking lot of the building Tyrell Suggs was watching that moment.

He sat there, his car seat reclined a bit, his window down, an elbow hanging out, enjoying the sunny day. He quizzed himself as he pulled from a needle joint he had rolled last night just in case he found himself in this exact situation—waiting with nothing else to do.

Blowing smoke out the window, his head spinning just a little, he wondered did Paul have a drug problem? The times Tyrell Suggs saw him, he looked straight, not like no fiend, but druggies had a way of hiding that shit well. He pulled the last little bit of smoke from the burned down roach, flicked it out the window, then gripped the nob to raise his seatback when he saw Paul exit the rehab center. He turned the key on the ignition, fired up the old Chevy engine, shifted the car in gear, and prepared to follow Paul again when he saw him pulling out the parking lot.

But Tyrell Suggs pushed the gear lever back in, and cut the engine.

He had a sneaking suspicion that what he really looked for was not with Paul, but inside that building.

After winding up the windows on the old car, he locked it, trotted across the street, and pulled open the doors of the rehab center. Old memories washed over him. The place looked the same as it did twenty years ago: mix-matched chairs, sitting atop a scarred up, dingy hardwood floor. A makeshift reception counter sat just left of the entry doors—the same table that had always been there.

Tyrell Suggs walked over. An aging white man, nearing sixty-five if he was a day, wore a too-big denim shirt, buttoned to the top of his narrow, wrinkled neck. His head bobbed, for he was near falling asleep.

Tyrell Suggs stared at the man a moment, shook his head, smiled, then slapped a hand down hard on the table, frightening the man out of his sleep and almost out his chair.

"Wake up, old man!" Tyrell Suggs yelled.

Attendees from the last meeting, easily a dozen of them looked over their shoulders to see what interrupted the after-meeting ritual of complimentary day-old donuts and red punch.

The old man glared, balloon-eyed at Tyrell Suggs, the brownish whites of his eyes widened with fear, until recognition covered his face, giving way to a smile.

"You almost scared me to death, Tyrell." The man stood, slowly made his way around the table.

Tyrell Suggs hugged him, clapped him on the back several times, sincerely happy to see him.

"Twenty years and you still doing this, Mr. Leonard. Go home, man."

"This is home," Mr. Leonard said. "Might as well get a few bucks, checking folks in between naps." Hunched over, Mr. Leonard slowly made his way back around the table and sat. "Don't tell me you here cause you back on something, are you, son?"

"Naw," Tyrell Suggs said. "But it never hurts to come back, get some reinforcement, and see some old friends. Thinking about sitting in for the next meeting. It's in fifteen minutes, right?"

"Ain't nothing change," Mr. Leonard smiled. "You know you still gotta sign in." He pushed a clipboard with a stack of old sign-in sheets clamped to it across the table toward Tyrell Suggs.

"Of course." Tyrell Suggs took the board, lifted the pen that was roped to it, but instead of signing his name to the fresh sheet that lay atop all the others, he lifted the page and scanned the names of the people who attended the last meeting. His eyes fell almost to the bottom when they stopped on a name—Shayla Taylor.

Tyrell Suggs looked toward the people standing in the large meeting room. There were eight men, four women, two of which were white, one a Latino, the last person, a sister.

"Bingo," Tyrell Suggs said under his breath. "Hello, Shayla Taylor, daughter of Mr. Paul Taylor."

20

Larry stood looking out one of Shreeva's condo windows. The sky was blue and cloudless, the sun warmed his face, but Larry frowned. He wore silk pajama bottoms, slippers, and an open silk robe, exposing his bare torso.

He shouldn't have felt as bad as he did. There had been good news last night. On the other end of the cell phone pressed to his ear—a finger stuffed in the opposite ear so that he could hear what was said over the laughter, chatter and loud music playing at the bar at the restaurant he sat in—Larry heard Tyrell Suggs tell him that he had some information for him.

"Hold on. Give me a second," Larry said, standing from the stool of the crowded bar that flew a rainbow colored flag outside its door. He turned to the man that had been sitting next to him, that man wearing a tight tank t-shirt and tight cut-off denim jeans.

"Save that seat for me?" Larry mouthed to him. The man smiled, patted the stool with a hand, and mouthed back, "Sure thing."

Outside, Larry walked up Tenth Street, stopping at the corner of Piedmont Avenue. "What did you find?"

"The daughter," Tyrell Suggs said, sounding proud of himself. "The boy led me right to her at a drug treatment facility."

"So he was lying about not having seen her?"

"He was."

"How do you know it was his daughter? Did you actually see her?"

"Did one better. Walked over, chatted her up, laughed a little, then she started spilling all her shit, said her dad was giving her a hard time, that he just came back into her life, but was really trying to make up for lost time. She was dude's daughter all right. What we gonna do now?"

There on the street corner, Larry standing behind a young black couple waiting for the walk signal, holding the hand of their young child, Larry remembered when Jabari was around the age of the little boy standing just in front of him, when he and Marian were so in love, and—"

"Bishop? You there?"

"Yeah, yeah," Larry said, blinking away the memory. "I'm here."

"You know what you wanna do next?"

"Not yet, but I'll know soon. Just be ready."

Larry disconnected the call, then saw Shreeva's name flashing on the screen.

He didn't want to speak with her. They hadn't worked things out after she made her demands regarding their potential marriage—after she got Super Black Woman on him, rolling her eyes, hand gesturing him to death, pointing fingers and waving arms. They had been avoiding each other in the condo, Shreeva going to bed early, getting up early and getting out the house before Larry even rolled out of bed.

The phone continued to ring in his hand. His thumb hovered over the IGNORE key, but he knew he would have to deal with her at some time. Her place was where he laid his head now, the only place he had left.

"Hello," Larry said, feeling all his muscles tighten.

"Are we still getting married, or have those plans changed because of everything you're going through?"

She didn't even say hello. Just got to it, Larry thought, grinding his teeth, shaking his head, wanting to throw the phone across the street.

"Shreeva, baby, I said I'm gonna marry you. We gonna do that," Larry said, starting back toward the bar. "But I got a lot of stuff going on right now and—"

"I know that. But that ain't got nothing to do with me. You not marrying me ain't gonnna make any of that magically disappear."

"And marrying you will?"

"No, but we're a team. As husband and wife, your problems won't just be yours, but ours."

Standing in front of the bar's open bay windows, Larry zoned off while Shreeva continued trying to sell marriage to him. At the same time, tank t-shirt guy was staring Larry down from inside the restaurant, drinking from a glass, rolling the straw across his tongue, then grabbing it and running his two fingers up and down the length of the narrow tube.

"Shreeva, I don't have time for this right now," Larry said, interrupting wherever she was in her rant.

"Dammit, Larry! How long have I—"

Larry disconnected the call, pushed the buttons it took to mute incoming calls and messages, slid the phone into his pocket and stepped back into the bar, taking the seat beside the man he was pretty sure he'd be going home with later.

Standing at Shreeva's window now, he heard her in the kitchen, opening and closing the fridge, going through the silverware drawer; she must not have had to go in work till late today.

Larry had slept on the couch last night. He didn't want to hear Shreeva's mouth the moment he set his head down on the pillow. It was almost four in the morning, and he felt it would've been damn disrespectful climbing into the bed of the woman that was dying to marry him, when he just spent the last few hours, drinking, shooting up drugs and fucking raw (Larry believed his name was Bret) the man he had met in the bar.

"Larry."

He turned around to see Shreeva standing behind him. Dressed for work, she wore a lavender dress, a white blazer over it. Her purse over her shoulder, she held an unopened cup of yogurt and spoon in her hand. She looked sad, disappointed and frustrated.

"Yeah," Larry said.

"What are you doing?" She asked, seeming to suggest whatever it had been, it was terribly wrong.

"I don't know what you mean."

"You came in at four this morning. I know things are hard right now, and I've been hard on you. I..." She set down her purse and yogurt on the dining room table, walked over, hugged him, kissed his face and rubbed his beard. "I want to tell you I'm sorry for being that way. I've waited for you all this time, and I thought about it, I can wait a little longer if you need me to. But I need to know that you aren't out there doing more of what landed you in the emergency room—doing something that could put us both at risk."

He knew exactly what she was saying. It was okay that he fucked dudes, it just needed to be under her supervision, and it needed to be done safely, with his shit strapped up tight.

"You aren't putting both of us at risk, are you?"

"I would never do that."

"Because there are things I can accept, and there are things I'll do for you, no questions asked, but I won't risk my life for you…at least not like that. I would rather not have you, than to do that." She kissed him softly on the lips. "You understand, baby?"

Larry looked her straight in the eyes, nodded his head, silent.

Shreeva smiled, grabbed her things from the table, started toward the front door, then stopped and turned back.

"Didn't know if I wanted to tell you this, but I guess I should."

"What is it?" Larry asked, unsettled.

"Mayor Bonner, he was at the restaurant yesterday, fucking siting at the table like a bear chewing on a steak, looking like he wished it was me. He said he heard word that you were getting a divorce, and asked if you were staying at my place. I hope you don't mind that I told him yes. It's the truth, but I also thought it would stop his fat ass from coming over here, trying to get some more sex."

Of course Bonner heard of the divorce, Larry thought. That was the only news about him that was being aired anymore, that, and his fiery fall from grace—news of his church no longer being his.

"It's fine," Larry said. "I'm glad you told him. You shouldn't have to worry about him coming over here anymore."

"Thank you, baby," Shreeva said, blowing him a kiss before she left him for work.

Larry turned back toward the window, looked down at the city below him, the city filled with tens of thousands of people that used to love him. Now it appeared there was just one left, and he seemed bent on doing everything imaginable to drive her away.

Maybe he should just forget about his family—let them go since they were struggling so hardily to tear away from him. And while he was at it, he could forget about Paul, too, and the revenge he sought against him. He could accept that things were the way they are, no matter how much he disliked that fact. He could quiet all the demons in his head, do as Shreeva asked, marry her and live happily ever after, forgetting about all the nonsense he struggled with now. He told himself he would think about that, and he thought to sit down, do it that very moment when a knock came at the condo door.

A smile came to his face, thinking that maybe Shreeva had forgotten her keys. She did that sometimes.

Larry walked to the door, a bounce in his step, actually thinking that he'd ask her if she could call in sick. It was a beautiful day. They could walk in the park, take in a movie and get lunch on a patio somewhere, maybe even talk more about them getting married.

Larry opened the door, the smile wider on his face, when he saw that it was not Shreeva who had knocked, but Mayor Bonner.

"Bishop." The big man smiled. Dressed in a business suit, he must've read the surprise on Larry's face. "Expecting someone else? Maybe your hot little piece of ass," Bonner said, stepping into the condo without permission. He walked past Larry. "That's some good pussy. You know I know from first hand experience."

Bonner turned to Larry, a bejeweled, sausage-fingered hand on his belly. "But then again you know that. Hell, you arranged it!" He laughed.

"What the fuck do you want, Bonner?" Larry said, closing the door. "Business between us is done. You got everything you wanted, so why the fuck am I looking at you?"

"Just thought I'd give you a heads up. A detective from the Atlanta PD came asking questions about some kid dying in the hospital from some beating—a kid you supposedly knew—one of your old spiritual sons."

"Why would he come looking for you?"

"Maybe because I saw news of the boy's death on TV. Maybe because I saw that there's was an investigation being opened and I figured they might consider you a likely suspect, and if they didn't, I wanted to let them know they should seriously consider it."

"Exactly what does that mean?" Larry said.

"That means I'm handing over the records of your drug arrest to this fine officer of the law, and will tell him whatever truths I know, and possibly a lie or two in order for him to charge you with the murder of that poor young man."

"Bonner, we had a deal! I give you the church, you don't press charges against me."

"And I'm upholding that deal, Bishop," Bonner said, pulling an unlit cigar from his suit jacket pocket, sliding it under his nose and breathing in its scent. "You know I still can't kiss my wife in the mouth. Each time I try, I see her sucking the dick of that gorilla of yours. I can see she knows that's in my head. She's embarrassed and ashamed because of it, but I just can't help it."

"You gave me your fucking word!"

"I'm not pressing charges against you, Larry," Bonner said, his voice taking on a much more serious tone. "I'm just doing everything in my power to have your black, country ass, locked away for life."

Larry's chest heaving, the muscles jumping in his clenched jaws, he said, "You don't want to go down this road with me. There will be nothing but hurt and heartache there. I beg you, for your own good, don't do this, Mayor Bonner. Nothing good can ever come of it."

Bonner shoved the cigar between his lips, lit the tip with a gold Zippo lighter he pulled from his trousers pocket, puffed from it and said, "You wearing an orange jumper with 'Department of Corrections' stamped on your back sounds like a whole hell of a lot of good to me." He walked past Larry toward the door. "Good day, Bishop Lakes."

21

Another week had passed without Larry seeing his children, but it wasn't for lack of asking. Unfortunately, Marian would no longer pick up his phone calls.

Half a dozen times, he stood outside the security gate of what was now Marian's mansion. He would yell into the intercom, demanding her to let him see the kids. Most times Marian wouldn't even respond. Once, Larry's mother-in-law's voice came out the tiny box, telling him if he didn't get out from in front of their house, she would call some thugs to remove him.

Larry left. Not for fear of what Estelle threatened, but because he still had other issues to deal with.

When he returned the following day, asking again, Marian came on the intercom and told Larry if he harassed them one more time, she would take out a restraining order.

He didn't need any more interaction with the law, any more paperwork filed against him relating in any way with the justice system. Bonner and Vernon, the APD detective, were still trying to pin Urail's murder on him.

So Larry stopped going to the house, and instead, resorted to parking outside of the kid's school, catching glimpses of them when they were allowed outdoors for recess and lunch.

Everyday over the past week, sitting in Tyrell Suggs's car, seeing Jabari or Simone for just a minute or two out the day, he wondered what they thought of their father. He wondered what Marian had told them, if they thought he abandoned them.

Breathing angrily behind the wheel of the car, infuriated he was in the position he was in, Larry would force himself to calm and focus on the priorities at hand—teaching Paul a lesson for toying with his family.

After Tyrell Suggs located Paul's daughter, it had taken Larry a day to determine just how he wanted to use her, but he figured it out.

The plan wouldn't be pretty, but it wasn't meant to be. The results would be ugly, gruesome, no less—the end outcome meant to make Paul wish he had never met Larry, had never stepped in and tried to take ownership of what wasn't his.

"Do you think you can get next to her?" Larry asked Tyrell Suggs the day after he had found the girl.

"Hell," Tyrell Suggs said. "The way she was all open, talking about everything, laughing with me, I was about to ask her ass out for a drink. But I know not to mix business with pleasure."

Larry thought a moment. "Ask her if you think she'll go. Ask her out."

"Then what?"

"Show her a nice time. Don't push too hard, but make it known you want to see her again. Try to get her to trust you."

"Cool. Not a problem," Tyrell Suggs said.

From what he told Larry, the girl was just 19 years old, tall, slender but very shapely. Her skin was the color of cherry wood, with lips, as Tyrell Suggs put it, "Could suck a basketball through a soda straw."

"Her mother is dead of an overdose," Tyrell Suggs told Larry after Shayla hung out with him three nights in a row. "She said Paul wanted her to come stay in his little apartment, but she wouldn't go. Told him she'd rather live in the shelter because she knew he would try to act the strict daddy and keep tabs on her. She's a rebellious bitch, Bishop. And she can drink her ass off."

Larry took the information gratefully, believing it would be easier than he thought to see his plan all the way though.

"Have you gotten sexual with her?" Larry asked Tyrell.

"Naw. Wasn't gonna do that unless I knew that was the direction you wanted me to take it."

"Have you had the opportunity? Do you think you can?"

There was a pause on the phone. "I think, maybe if I get her drunk enough."

"I see," Larry said, contemplating. "What drug was she addicted to? Did she say?"

"Her thing was meth."

Larry thought about the chunk of heroin he still had. He hadn't sold any of it as he intended. His heart wasn't in it as he thought it would've been. He had received a couple of calls from a number he didn't recognize — the number he believed belonged to Jayteesh, the man who gave the drugs to Larry on consignment.

Those calls he ignored, knowing he would have to deal with the man and the threats he made about what would happen if Larry hadn't gotten his money to him by the due date. If Larry was correct, that date had passed two days ago, but there were more important things Larry was concerned with now.

"Do you think she'd like heroin?"

"She's an addict, Bishop. She'll do any drug she can get her hands on. I guarantee you that," Tyrell Suggs said then.

And now, five days after Tyrell Suggs made that promise, Larry pulled up in front of his house, behind a Ford SUV.

Larry stepped out of the Toyota, strolled across Tyrell's Suggs's freshly cut lawn then climbed the stairs and rang the doorbell. He glanced out at the truck, believing it belonged to Tyrell Suggs's nephews, Clinton and Travis, both around twenty years old.

Tyrell Suggs pushed open the security gate, a video camera in his hand.

"Is it happening?" Larry asked.

"Think you ought to see for yourself," Tyrell Suggs said, closing the door.

He led Larry through the house, toward a guess bedroom.

"She was trippin a little at first, but once the drug kicked in, mixed with the alcohol, she was game like a fucking professional."

As Larry walked down the hall, nearing the bedroom door, he heard the feminine moans and masculine grunts, the curses made during sex—the banging of the headboard and the whining of the bedsprings.

Tyrell Suggs grabbed the doorknob. "You ready?"

Larry didn't answer at first, not as eager to see this as he thought he would've been, not as happy to know that he had succeeded in corrupting this child, when not long ago, one of his missions was to save people like this. He wished this hadn't had to happen, but Paul in all his arrogant foolishness forced his hand.

"Yeah, I'm ready," Larry said.

Tyrell Suggs punched the record button on the camera and pushed open the door.

What Larry saw inside was as shocking as he hoped it wouldn't have been.

On top the twin size bed was Paul's daughter, as gorgeous as Tyrell Suggs described her, butt naked and beautiful, long black hair pinned up in a bun atop her head, so as not to get in the way as she performed very skillful looking oral sex on one of the boys. One boy stood at the head of the bed, shirtless, his jeans and boxers dropped around the heels of his Polo boots, his head thrown back as he grabbed tight to Sayla's head.

On the foot end of the bed, the other boy, dressed similarly, held onto the girl's round, plump ass cheeks, as he banged her from behind.

"This dick good, bitch?" the boy in back—Larry believed to be Clinton—said.

"Mmmm, hmmmm," Shayla moaned around a mouthful of dick.

"Then say it, bitch!" Clinton demanded.

Shayla pulled Travis's penis from her mouth, without missing a beat, continued to stroke it, looking over her shoulder at Clinton. "This is good dick, baby! Good ass dick!"

"Obedient as a fucking dog," Tyrell Suggs whispered.

Larry sadly nodded. "You getting all this?"

Tyrell Suggs tilted the camera a bit so Larry could see the tiny monitor.

"Yup. Wouldn't want dear old dad to miss a thing," Tyrell Suggs said.

22

When Larry left, the poor girl was sprawled out on the bed, hands and feet hanging out over all four corners, mouth open, drool spilling over her lips. The boys stood over her, pulling their t-shirts over their heads, giving each other dap on a self-proclaimed, job well done. They hugged their uncle and thanked him for the experience.

"If you ever got anything like this going again, Unc, you know where you can find us," the older boy, Clinton said.

Tyrell Suggs laughed, smiling like a proud father watching his sons score their first touchdown.

"See you later, Uncle Larry," Travis said.

Larry nodded to both boys, waved as they walked out the room, down the hall and then out the house. Afterward, Larry glanced back down at Shayla. The only indication that she was alive and had not overdosed, was that she snored.

"What are you gonna do with her?" Larry asked, so very grateful that wasn't his daughter lying there.

"I'll let her rest a while," Tyrell Suggs said. "When she wakes up, I'll probably take my turn on her. You saw how good she was throwing that pussy, didn't you Bishop?"

"I saw," Larry said, not nearly as happy about what he just witnessed as Tyrell Suggs appeared.

"I mean, you don't mind do you?"

Larry shook his head. "Do whatever you want with her, but I need a copy of that," Larry said, nodding to the video camera.

"Definitely," Tyrell Suggs said. "Give me a minute, and I'll burn it to a disc for you."

Before driving back to Shreeva's, Larry made a stop at the mansion. He thought of calling Marian, having her come out so he could hand the DVD to her, personally see the look on her face when he told her what was on it, but he figured Marian wouldn't answer his call after their last meeting.

He slipped the DVD into the mail, knowing she would get it when she checked the box for the evening delivery. It would be one more thing in which she'd never forgive him.

On the way to Shreeva's, Larry was still disturbed by what happened with Shayla—no child should have to endure something like that—but the thought of seeing his mistress actually made him feel just a bit better about everything.

He had been thinking more about the point she had consistently tried to make—that things would be easier for him, and better for them both, if they were to just marry. Like she said, they would be a team, and Larry figured if the woman wanted that so much, was fighting so hard to help him carry the backbreaking load he had been shouldering, why not allow her?

Last night, Shreeva told him she wanted to make him something special to show how much she valued him, and how well he had been managing all of the nonsense that had been happening.

Obviously, she hadn't known about his daily visits to his children's school and his plans to seek revenge against Paul and Mayor Bonner, and Larry figured there was no need to inform her. Revenge against Bonner would be much worse than what just went down with Paul's daughter. It would have enormous impact—and a much higher price would be paid—so Larry wanted Shreeva taking no part in, or having no knowledge of that.

The plan had yet to be executed.

Larry was waiting for Tyrell Suggs to get back to him with the person willing to do the kind of job Larry needed done for drugs—another chunk of the heroin Larry had been given—since he really had no money to pay.

Five minutes from Shreeva's, Larry's cell rang. He picked it up from the passenger seat, checked the number, thinking that it might have been Shreeva, or maybe Jayteesh calling again, bugging him about his money. The man had left three threatening messages already on Larry's voicemail—something about blowing his head off when he found him.

The call came from neither Shreeva, nor Jayteesh, but from Bret, the man Larry met last week at the bar. Larry punched the IGNORE button and set the phone back down.

He had seen Bret almost a half dozen times since the first day—Bret becoming the outlet Van had been. He knew he needed to stop seeing the man, for never once had they used a condom. But that wasn't the only reason Bret had to go. Larry was tired of lying to Shreeva. Since the talk, Shreeva telling Larry she would no longer pressure him—just be there for him whenever he was ready, he had been feeling tremendous guilt, telling her he was being faithful, when there was nothing further from the truth.

He realized if he were to get serious with the girl, give her what she was asking, had always wanted, he would have to get rid of Bret, and whatever other pieces of sex Larry had been sliding up in.

Funny thing was, Larry thought as he parked the car in front of Shreeva's condo building, he believed he was okay with that. Maybe it was all the hell he was going through. Maybe it took losing almost everything for him to realize just what he had in Shreeva. Whatever it was, Larry believed now, after fifteen years, he could finally do right by the woman.

Walking down the hallway that led to Shreeva's condo, Larry wished now that he had did as he first planned, stopped at the local Publix grocery store and bought some wine for dinner. It would've been a nice gesture, would've let Shreeva know he was appreciative of her cooking for him, and the patience she showed in dealing with him.

But he hadn't, because when he called to ask what kind she wanted, she hadn't picked up. He left a message, tried her again, but still Shreeva hadn't answered, and she hadn't called him right back, as she normally did.

At the condo door, Larry slid his key into the lock, pushed the door, but was surprised when it refused to open more than a couple of inches. He looked up, saw the security catch was on, stopping it from opening.

Shreeva only used that lock at night when both he and she were inside, but she never engaged it before Larry had gotten home. Was she still worried about Bonner showing up, forcing his way in? Could he have been in there now?

Larry knocked on the door, trying to slow the dreadful thoughts that started to fill his head. He called through the opening. "Shreeva, it's Larry. You okay in there?"

He heard talking, hushed whispering.

"Shreeva!" He called again. "Open the door! I said are you okay?"

Larry stepped back. Pulled his phone out, thought of dialing her, but remembered she hadn't picked up before, realized maybe that was because Bonner stopped her.

He lowered his shoulder, threw himself against the door, pounding it hard. The lock nor the door gave at all.

He pressed his face into the open space, and called again. "Shreeva!"

"Hold on, hold on!" A woman's voice called. It wasn't Shreeva's.

"Who is that?" Larry said, worried, not knowing just what the hell was going on.

"I said hold on!"

The door closed, the lock was disengaged and it opened again.

Standing in the doorway was a woman, short, wide-hipped, a freshly sewn in weave flowing shiny over her shoulders. This was Shreeva's best friend, Connie. They were friends long before Shreeva hooked up with Larry, Larry rarely seeing Connie since Shreeva appreciated how much the two couldn't stand each other.

"Where's Shreeva?" Larry said, stepping forward, Connie stepping in front of him, not letting him pass. "And why the hell was the lock on?"

Connie stared hatefully at Larry. "You filthy motherfucker!"

"What did you say?" Larry asked, but decided he wouldn't bother with whatever nonsense Connie was talking, for he still didn't know what was going on with Shreeva. He tried to move past Connie, but she had the nerve, the audacity and the lack of common sense to press a hand into Larry's chest to hold him back.

"Woman, if you don't let me past, I swear—"

"Let him go, Connie," Shreeva said, finally emerging from the hallway. She wore a robe over a tank and sweatpants, her hair tangled and tied behind her head with a scarf. She neared them, walking slowly.

Larry noticed her eyes were pink, her lids puffy, as though she had been crying—was still crying. But that was not all. In either of her hands she dragged two large suitcases.

"What…what the hell is going on?" Larry asked, looking around the condo as though still not certain it was just the three of them there.

"Shreeva needs to be asking your nasty, stank-ass that," Connie said, her nose wrinkled up like Larry looked and smelled worse than the names she called him.

"What the fuck are you talking about?" Larry asked Connie, then turned to Shreeva. "What is she saying? Why are you carrying your suitcases? Where are you going?"

"Those her suitcases, but they packed for you, motherfucker!" Connie said, swinging her arm in a wide arc, her finger landing on Larry. "You the one who leaving."

"Shreeva, what is—"

"I had been having some discomfort when going," Shreeva said, her words low. She dabbed the corner of her eyes with a wad of crumpled Kleenex. "I thought nothing of it. My annual was coming in a couple of days, told myself it was probably a yeast infection…I'd get something for it. They ran some tests…" More tears flowed from Shreeva's eyes, scaring Larry.

What was she saying? Discomfort when she went to the bathroom? Tests? His head swam, fearing the possibilities of what she was about to tell him.

"They came back positive for gonorrhea, Larry."

"You nasty ass motherfucker!" Connie said again. "After all my girl has done for you, the way she loved you. Was it a man, a woman or a boy this time, Larry?"

"I...I didn't do it," Larry said, sounding uncertain. He reached out to Shreeva. She recoiled in fear, dropping the suitcases, stumbling backward.

"Get away from her!" Connie snapped.

"Shreeva, I didn't do this!" Larry appealed, praying that there was truth in what he was saying. But at the same time, if it had been him, he tried to determine who was responsible for infecting him. Van? Jayteesh? Bret? It could've been any of them, because Larry was foolish enough to slide up in all of them raw.

"I knew you didn't love me enough to stop," Shreeva said. "But you didn't even care enough to protect yourself. Didn't care that you could've given me some shit like this!" Shreeva said. "How could you?"

It was everything that was happening to him, but hadn't he told her that, hadn't he used that excuse over and over again already? "I swear, baby. I—"

"Get out, Larry, and don't ever come back," Shreeva said, tears crawling down her face, exhaustion and frustration dragging her shoulders and head down. She looked as though she was about to fall to the floor.

"Shreeva, baby, please," Larry begged.

"I said go!" She shrieked hysterically, her voice so loud, Larry was startled into silence, and only then did he truly realize the irreparable damage he had done.

He looked soberly around the room—the space they shared for so many years, the space they were supposed to have shared for many more— as though he'd never see it again.

His eyes settled upon the suitcases. One had fallen over sideways. He reached down to grab them.

"That's right motherfucker, pick those up, and get the fuck out of here!" Connie said. She stood beside Shreeva, an arm around her, protecting her from the man that had hurt her for the last time.

Larry grabbed the cases, dragged them a short length then looked back to Shreeva, prepared to make a last appeal.

"Keep it moving, nigga," Connie said. "And ain't no need to come back. Whatever you left here, we'll send to your ass, or we can just throw away."

Larry lugged the cases to the door, opened it, then over his shoulder, without looking back, he said, "Just throw it away."

23

Tyrell Suggs brought the car to a skidding halt in front of the Atlanta Rehabilitation center, thankful no one was hanging outside. If that had been the case, he would've had to speed on, stop in some deserted grassy lot, or in some alley behind a vacant building and take care of the business that needed tending to.

He threw open his car door, hurried around to the passenger side, pulling that door open and frantically reaching inside. This wasn't supposed to be happening. All he wanted was his turn, get a little piece of that good shit the young girl was throwing around.

She had given it good to his nephews; she was fully engaged, acted as though she wanted nothing more than to do her job and please whoever wanted pleasing. But after the boys left, and after Tyrell Suggs took the time to burn a copy of the video for Bishop, Shayla started coming down from her high.

When he stepped back in the room, stripped off his clothes and tried to climb on top of the girl, he felt her resisting him, pushing him back, as if to throw him from onto of her.

"C'mon, baby," Tyrell Suggs said, pressing his lips to hers — attempting to smother her with kisses, and at the same time slide a finger between her thighs to get her more in the mood.

Shayla whipped her head about, her eyes still closed, spitting the kisses he gave from her lips.

He straddled her, held her down by her wrists, remembering how sensual she was when being taken by his nephews. He would have her the same way, even if he had to take it.

But as he continued forcing himself on her, she fought back harder, lifting one of her legs, trying to gouge her knee into his crotch.

Tyrell Suggs dodge her assaults then jumped off of her, a hand raised, ready to beat the girl into submission. Then he remembered there were still drugs left.

Moments later, a tourniquet cinched around Shayla's arm as she squirmed to free herself from the elaborate hold Tyrell Suggs had on her— he managed to push the drug into her system.

Within seconds the drug took hold and the fight left her. Her eyes rolled up, showing white. Her body went limp, and she fell backward onto the bed, her full, wet lips parting slightly.

"Good girl," Tyrell Suggs said, reaching over, undoing the band from around her arm, tossing it over the side of the bed. He mounted her, pushed her thighs open with his knees, and slid into her.

Warm and wet, she felt better than Tyrell Suggs could've imagined.

He lowered his face, kissed her again. This time instead of turning away, he felt her welcome him, wrap her lips around his tongue. He thought he would bust that moment. He held on, telling himself he was going to wear her ass out, give her the best fucking of her young life, have her knocking on his door begging for more, when suddenly she started to cough, a little at first, then brutally.

He ignored her, pushing deeper into her wetness, sliding out and in again, believing the coughing fit would pass, but when she started convulsing violently —her head and torso leaping from the mattress, her arms flailing, her legs thrashing about as though she had been struck by lightening, he withdrew from her.

Tyrell Suggs fell away, staggered backward, watching, eyes big, as she writhed about the mattress, then fell to the floor, thudding around, the palms of her hands, the soles of her feet, slapping the hardwood. A moment later, she lay still.

"Girl?" Tyrell Suggs called to her, cautiously taking a step toward her, peering around the bed to see her lying on her side, one arm folded behind her back, the other stretched up overhead as if to reach something under the bed.

"Shayla," he said, bending to one knee, rolling her over, looking down at her to see her staring back at him. Surprised at first, he fell backward again from shock. But when he saw that she wasn't moving, he pressed his fingers into her neck, feeling for a pulse. There was a beat, but so faint he could barely detect it.

"Fuck!" Tyrell Suggs said, quickly getting to his feet. He spun two circles, looking about the room as if for instructions on how to handle this. Of course there were none.

Seeing her jeans lying across a chair back, he snatched them, threw himself down over Shayla's body again, grabbed one of her ankles and forced her foot into the leg of the jeans.

Now, outside of the Atlanta Rehabilitation Center, Tyrell Suggs pulled Shayla's limp body from the car, and from under her arms, he dragged her across the pavement. He laid her gently at the front door, careful to set her head down, looking at her beautiful face one last time.

"Damn, sorry 'bout that, girl," Tyrell Suggs said. "Wish I could've done more, but 911 is gonna have to do."

He punched the numbers into his phone, and as he hurried around the car, he said, "Hello. I need to report an overdose!"

24

The sky was dark outside. The streetlamps flickered on as Larry stood in Shreeva's condo parking lot, unable to believe what had just happened, unable to believe she accused him of giving her a venereal disease.

As he hoisted the suitcases filled with what he imagined were the belongings he brought to her place over the years, he questioned how could he have given her something if he wasn't infected? He wasn't itching down there. It didn't burn when he took a piss.

"The woman don't know what she's talking about," Larry mumbled, slamming the trunk closed. But as he walked around the Toyota, he knew Shreeva wouldn't have accused him of such a thing if she weren't certain.

But there was a chance it wasn't Larry at all.

He had given her permission to have sex with other men. Possibly one of them burned her. He thought about that scenario a moment, actually hoped that it had gone down that way, but Larry knew Shreeva was meticulous about having the random men she slept with use protection.

He did it. He was the guilty one.

Larry slid the key in the car door, telling himself he needed to get to somebody's emergency room, get tested and get a prescription for whatever Shreeva said Larry gave her. After the drug did its job and he was cured, he'd go back to her, tell her how sorry he was and that he was no longer interested in playing games. They could still get married, still be that team she had spoken so much about.

Larry pulled open the car door preparing to climb in, when another car pulled to a screeching halt beside him. Startled, Larry spun to see a black Audi S5, idling so close that it was nearly touching his pant leg.

The car's windows, tinted black, Larry had no idea of who was inside. One powered down, bass heavy music pouring out, assaulting Larry's ears.

"Bishop, how you doin?" Jayteesh said, leaning out. He wore dark sunglasses, a sheer smoke colored stocking cap over his head, the flattened pink Mohawk visible underneath.

How did the dealer knew where Larry lived? How did he find him?

Jayteesh turned his music down, but it remained loud enough to require the two men raise their voices to be heard.

"I've been calling you," Jaytessh said. "You ignoring my calls?"

"I was gonna call—" Larry started.

"About my drugs? About the money you were supposed to have already delivered to me?"

"Yeah."

"Then it's a good thing I'm here. Why don't you go in the trunk of that piece of shit car and get my money, Bishop."

Larry looked to the back of the Toyota like the money might've actually been there, then admitted, "I don't have it."

"Bishop, Bishop," Jayteesh said, reaching over and turning the radio volume all the way down. "Get in. We need to talk."

"Why?" Larry said, suddenly frightened of this man.

"I just motherfucking told you," Jayteesh said, pointing the barrel of a huge caliber pistol, suddenly appearing from nowhere, at Larry.

Jayteesh opened his door, set a foot on the ground—he wore pink flip-flops—and started to get out, raising the gun, pointing it between Larry's eyes.

Larry quickly made his way round the car, pulled the door open, lowered himself into the leather seat.

Jayteesh raised his window, sealing them inside, then turned to Larry. "The time I gave you to sell those drugs been passed. You got my money or not? And I need you to think very carefully about how you answer."

Sadly, Larry said, "I told you. I haven't been able to sell—"

"It don't got to be money you made off the drugs. I don't give a fuck if you sold them or not. If you got enough in an account at Chase Bank, or whatever institution that keeps your fucking money, if you got it in a safe at the church, I'll take it," Jayteesh said, pulling something from the center armrest compartment of the car.

Larry had no idea of what that was, until he saw the man screwing, what Larry realized was a silencer onto the barrel of the gun.

Larry looked out the windshield, hoping there was someone in the parking lot, someone to witness what was happening—what might've been about to happen. No one.

"The money, Bishop. I ain't fucking playing! You got it or you don't?"

Larry had taken a moment to answer, pulling air deep into his lungs, holding it a
moment, exhaling, then giving the answer that surprised even himself.

"What'd you say to me?" Jayteeh said. After hearing Larry's response, he turned in his seat, squaring himself to face Larry, holding the gun with both hands now, the barrel just an inch from Larry's nose.

"I said I don't have it," he repeated. "I didn't sell the drugs and I don't' have it in no account. I don't have your money, Jayteesh. I just don't."

Jayteesh nodded several times. "Word. Word, word," he said actually smiling. "You owning that shit like a man. Ain't no crying or nothing. No lying, begging saying that you gonna get it. None of that 'please give me another day', shit. Word, Bishop!" Jayteesh said, pulling the gun down a second to screw tighter the silencer on the tip. "There's honor in that shit, you know that." The gun was pointing in Larry's face again, Jayteesh looking over the sight, one eye squinting as though aiming at something a hundred meters away and not right in front of him.

Larry trembled as cold sweat trickled from his brow and down the center of his spin. He was about to die and—

"You know what?" Jayteesh said, lowering the gun.

Larry exhaled, feeling like his hear was going to give.

"Because you being straight, I'm gonna give your ass an extension. Twelve more hours to find my money and—"

"Twelve hours won't matter," Larry said, realizing he was sealing his fate, if there ever had been any chance he was going to live through this ordeal. But he wasn't about to run around begging people for money to satisfy a piece of shit who, Larry figured, already had more money than he'd ever need. There was too many other things he had to do.

"I don't have your money now. Ain't ever gonna have it," Larry said.

"And the drugs?"

"Used most of them. No," Larry said, staring Jayteesh in the eyes. "I don't have them either."

"You's a frosty motherfucker, Bishop," Jayteesh said. "You saying you'd rather take this bullet I got for you, then to at least try and come up with the money?"

His church, his reputation, his children, his wife, now the girl that loved him—the woman that he could've seriously seen spending the rest of his life with was all gone.

"Do what you gotta do, Jayteesh," Larry said, realizing he had nothing left to live for.

"Cool," Jayteesh said, pressing the tip of the gun to Larry's head, and surprisingly, Larry felt himself pushing his head into the weapon, wishing Jayteesh would pull the trigger and get all of it over with.

Larry closed his eyes, started to pray, the words coming softly from his lips. He said goodbye to his children, his wife, said goodbye to Shreeva, and the rest of the people he loved, as he prepared to—

"Get the fuck out my car!" Jayteesh said.

So deep in prayer, Larry's eyes closed as he waited for the bullet to end his life, Jayteesh had to give the order a second time.

"I said, get the fuck out my car, motherfucker!"

Larry's eyes slowly opened. "What did you say?"

"I ain't fucking with you no more." Jayteesh lowered the gun for the last time to the armrest.

"And your money?" Larry asked.

"God must've spoke to me or some shit, told me to spare yo' ass, so we through," Jayteesh said, screwing the silencer off the gun. "Let me see your ass around that club again, on any of my corners, or anywhere near me, me and God will have to talk about this shit again. Now get the fuck out!"

25

Marian sat in the chair that used to belong to her husband, behind the desk that was once was his, in the office that she had discovered the horrors she would've never suspected him of. That video was why there were divorced papers being filed, why she would never again trust him with her children, and why there was another man already in line to take Larry's place.

No, Marian wasn't certain she'd marry Paul—and even though she told Larry that at their last meeting—she wasn't even sure she loved Paul enough yet to marry him, but what she did know was that he was a positive influence on the children; they loved him, and Paul loved them just as much. And unlike Larry, Paul was devoted, affectionate and trustworthy, among so many other things that Larry had stopped being so long ago.

But as Marian sat there, she noticed she was trembling, felt her stomach twisting as she eyed the thin, plastic DVD case she had pulled the disc from. That moment she wondered whether she had let Paul in too soon.

Only after viewing what was on that disc had she questioned if she knew everything there was to know about him? Questioned if she knew much of anything, other than what was on his resume when he was first presented to her?

She looked up at the big flat screen TV where she had just viewed the filth that Larry must've left in the mailbox for her. It was horrible footage of some girl being gang raped—at least that's what it looked like to Marian, although the girl seemed to be fully participating, gratefully taking in the boy behind her, as she pulled and sucked on the boy in front of her, then allowed them to switch positions and use her over again in the same awful, horrifying way.

That's how the tape started—the moment after Marian pressed play—sounds of grunting and moaning and passion filled cries accompanying images of black bodies writhing and contorting, hands massaging spit-shiny body parts. The remote jumped from Marian's hand, as she turned away, disgusted by what she saw. She bent down to retrieve it, pointed it at the screen when she heard another voice on the tape—a shockingly familiar voice. She waited a moment, wanting to avert her eyes from the terrible immorality of the video, but she needed to know who that voice belonged to, verify that she had been wrong about who she thought it might be. She sensed that person would soon reveal himself, step into the frame. And as she feared, the person she suspected appeared in front of the camera as if acting the reporter on the street, covering the scene behind him.

To Marian's dismay, Larry was there, staring solemnly at Marian, obscuring the animal behavior that was going on behind him, but having to speak loudly to be heard over the guttural noises that were produced from it.

"How does it feel, Paul, to have some man step in and mess with *your* child?" Larry looked over his shoulder, turned back to the camera, shaking his head—as though he wasn't the one that orchestrated that entire scene—disgusted by what he saw. Then he stepped away, and allowed whoever was filming to continue doing his job.

Marian stabbed the remote, clicking it off, freezing the images on the screen—both boys in mid thrust, the girl between them, open on both ends, looking thankful for what they gave her, when Marian knew couldn't have been remotely true.

Turning away from the TV, she felt she would vomit all over Larry's desk. She got up, wrapped her arms around herself. Nervously pacing the room, she thought to call Larry, find out just what the hell was going on, but told herself she wouldn't yet. She needed to find out why Larry mentioned Paul in the video, referring to "your child".

Paul had no children.

Marian had asked him that at one time or another, while lying in bed entangled in the others arms and legs, one of the first nights after they had just made love.

He said he always wanted kids, and that he thought he'd make a pretty good father, but no, he didn't have any.

Had he lied to her?

The possibility stopped Marian in the middle of the office, deep concern and building worry etched on her face. If he had lied about that, what else could he possibly be lying about?

She felt herself staring down at the ring Paul just gave her. She moved to pull it from her finger when she heard the downstairs door open and close, Paul calling out, "Hey everybody, I'm home."

There was happiness in his voice. He sounded more joyful now than he had in the short time she's known him. He sounded fulfilled, purposeful, as though all the goals he set forth to accomplish were right there in front of him, and he was well on his way to achieving them.

Marian started toward the office door, stopped herself, closed her eyes, her arms still wrapped around her torso, as if consoling herself for what she had just seen, and what was about to happen.

"Up here," she called, trying to sound as upbeat as he did, but knew she failed miserably.

She heard Paul bounding up the stairs, two at time, as energetically and happily as the kids would run down them when they knew something special awaited them on the first floor.

He stepped through the office door, and not noticing the somber mood, the dim lights, the TV on (little green light illuminated at the bottom corner of the set, but paused on a black screen) he took Marian's face in his hands, kissed her lips, hugging her.

"Ahhh," Paul exhaled. "Couldn't wait to get back to you."

Marian said nothing, wondering how long it would take him to notice she hadn't kissed him back, that her arms hung at her sides and she wasn't nearly as happy to see him as he said he was to see her. She wondered how long it would take him to realize there was some serious shit wrong.

He slowly pulled away from her, held her by the shoulders at arms length.

"Everything all right, baby?"

No need in tiptoeing, Marian thought. Might as well come out with hit.

"Do you have a child?" And before he could fix his mouth to say 'no'—Marian saw him ready to do just that—she said, "You need to be honest with me this time. You just need to be."

"Why are you asking me that?" Paul said, appearing all of sudden frightened.

"Answer the question, Paul!"

He shook his head as though telling himself it was foolish to tell truth, but realized he had no other choice.

"I'm sorry that I told you I didn't, but yes. I have a little girl. Well, not so little now. She's 19, but why are you—"

Before he could finish, Marian pulled away from him, went to the desk, picked up the remote and aimed it at the TV.

"You might want to prepare yourself for this."

Marian pressed the PLAY button. From the beginning, the DVD started, and as before, the moaning and pleasure laced curses oozed loud and obscenely from the speakers—the arched backs, sheet-clutching fists and sweat covered asses, stained the screen.

Marian hadn't heard it, or hadn't noticed it before, but this time she heard one of the men say the girl's name.

"Shayla!" he said, his hands disappearing into the teen's thick black hair as he pulled her head further into his groin. "Suck this big dick, Shayla. Suck this dick, girl!"

Marian's eyes were on Paul. He looked a shell of himself, as though he was made of matchsticks and was ready to fall to pieces that moment. His eyes wide, staring disbelievingly at the screen, chest heaving, shallow hurried breaths pushing through his open mouth, he looked like a crazed man about to commit murder.

"What is this?" Paul yelled. "Who sent this to—"

Before Marian could answer, her husband appeared on the screen again, asking that question. *"How does it feel, Paul, to have some man step in and mess with your child?"*

To Marian, it sounded like a question belonging to an unfinished conversation. And it started to come together for her that moment—Larry pissed about the access Paul had to his kids, then the news of the engagement. Was this retaliation for that? It had to have been.

"Give me the remote!" Paul said, snatching it out of Marian's hand. He pointed it, stopped the DVD from playing.

"Paul—" she thought to ask him why Larry would do such a thing, but she had already worked it out in her head.

Paul stormed across the room, jabbed the eject button on the DVD player, snatched the disc out, then broke it into pieces between his fists, throwing them to the ground.

"Where is he?" Paul said, scanning the room as if expecting Larry to pop out of a closet.

"Paul, don't do anything foolish," Marian said, grabbing him by his arms.

He took hold of her, forcefully enough for her to feel a bit of pain.

"Do you know where your husband is?" Paul said, speaking the words slowly, a short pause in between each, as though she was a child.

"No I don't, Paul. But I don't think you should do anything this moment. Just sit a minute."

He shut his eyes tight. She felt his body trembling, as though enduring some great pain, and she knew he was considering what she asked him. When he opened his eyes, they were cloudy with impending tears.

"I'm sorry, Marian," Paul said. And the murderous pain she saw just a moment ago was back, and it was so intense that she knew nothing short of killing her husband would ease his pain.

"He has to pay for this. Do you understand, Marian? I'm sorry, but he has to pay."

She watched the tears fall from his eyes as he stared down at her, then finally tore away.

26

"You sure you trying to do this, Bishop?" Tyrell Suggs asked Larry after pulling

up and shutting the Monte Carol off on the darkened residential street in Riverdale—a predominately black suburb south of Atlanta. The street was lined with project apartment buildings, two stories high, bars on the windows, and cars parked outside costing less than the huge wheels and tires they rode on.

"You know I can handle it for you," Tyrell Suggs told Larry. "I'll let you know when it's done. You don't need to be around this."

"I need to see it happen. I need to be the one that does it," Larry said, straightening in his seat, watching the man sitting in the white Dodge Challenger across the way, the tiny square glow of a cell phone cutting the darkness of the car's cabin. Larry assumed the driver was speaking to whomever he was going to visit inside the ratty project building he was parked in front of.

"The way his father has been hounding me, trying to pin that boy's murder on me, trying to put me in jail just because he doesn't like me—I need to be the one that does this," Larry said, seeming to assure himself more than Tyrell Suggs.

Yesterday, Marian had called Larry asking him if he actually had anything to do with Urail being beaten, giving him the news that recently detectives had been calling, asking questions. They had actually come by the house with a warrant, saying they needed to search Larry's office for anything that would help to find the boy's killer.

"The kids were home," Marian said, distraught, sounding as though Larry was to blame. "Jabari and Simone had to see all of that—police marching through our house like we were harboring a fugitive."

Larry tried to defend himself, told Marian he had nothing to do with what they were trying to prove him guilty of.

"Like you had nothing to do with molesting those boys?"

"I have to go, Marian," Larry said, ashamed.

Hanging up the phone, he told himself Bonner had finally taken things too far. It was brazen enough to lay his hands on a woman Larry loved. But then to plant false evidence on Larry, have him taken into custody and beaten, Bonner was foolishly playing with fire. But now he went as far to harass the family of a man who had nothing to lose, a man who did not blink when a gun was held to his head—Bonner had to realize retaliation would be brought against him in biblical proportion.

Still watching the Challenger, Larry saw the cell phone light go off.

"Should we get out now?" Larry asked Tyrell Suggs, never having done this before. "We don't want him to get away."

"It's cool," Tyrell Suggs said. "We got him." He reached across Larry and into the glove box, pulled out a big handgun he had hidden there. "You sure?" he asked again.

Larry nodded, trying to appear confident. He had handled a gun many times, fired them before but never at a person—never with intent to kill.

Tyrell Suggs set the gun in Larry's lap.

They exited the car, leaving the doors open, as not to make any more noise than was necessary, potentially drawing the man's attention to them; he was a cop and might've been carrying his gun under his civilian clothes.

Mayor's Bonner's son, the man that put drugs into Larry's car, dragged him, handcuffed into custody, starting Larry's decent down the steep mountain of pain, anguish and torment, walked at a normal pace toward the project building, as though he had not a care in the world—as though he wasn't responsible for destroying a man's life, responsible for taking away any and everything Larry ever loved. The junior Bonner, at least from behind, looked as though his conscious was clear, and that none of the actions he ever committed might have rubbed the wrong man the wrong way, having that man, one night, sneaking up behind him to make him pay for the horror caused by those actions.

Yes, tonight the man would pay, and Larry was surprised that he hadn't turned, hadn't sensed him and Tyrell Suggs just ten feet behind him.

Officer Bonner's cellphone rang, startling Larry.

Tyrell Suggs grabbed him by the arm, settling him with a look that conveyed confidence, a look that said Larry was capable of doing this no matter how much he might've doubted himself or how scared he might've been.

Bonner stopped to look down at his phone, then pressed it to his ear and continued walking. He laughed, and Larry thought that at least the boy had a moment of joy before he paid the ultimate price for both his and his father's foolishness.

Larry heard the Bonner boy say something about "…fucking this bitch I pulled over yesterday."

He laughed, sounding a lot like his father, which made Larry want to hurt the boy even more.

Only three feet behind Bonner, Larry looked to his friend, Tyrell Suggs nodding his head, his hand disappearing into his jacket pocket, probably reaching for his own gun just in case Larry choked—stared frightened at Bonner, unable to pull the trigger. That shit wasn't gonna happen. This would be the night Bonner would pay, and his father would feel the wrath of ever fucking with Larry.

"Officer Bonner..." Larry called, raising the gun shoulder height.

Mid laugh, Bonner turned around smiling, the cellphone still to his ear.

Larry paused just long enough for the officer to see exactly who was standing behind the gun pointed at him, long enough so Larry could see the expression of surprise—see the boy's eyes bulge, fill with the realization that the breath he just drew would be his last—long enough for Boner to process that he would die.

The gun went off twice in Larry's fists, spitting up orange fire as it expelled two bullets that sped through the air into Bonner's face, traveled through his brain, then exploded out the back of his skull. And as the boy fell, Larry turned the gun downward, shooting Bonner three more times in the chest, the boy's body jumping around on the pavement as it absorbed the sizzling lead.

Larry stood over the body, strangely calm, the gun still pointed at Bonner, wishing it was the boy's father.

"You good?" Tyrell Suggs asked, looking over his shoulder, not seeming terribly concerned that anyone heard the shots fired, for in this neighborhood, gunshots were heard as often as dogs barking.

"Yeah," Larry said.

"Then we best be going."

Larry felt hands on him.

He twisted and turned, unconsciously brushing them off, mumbling something in his sleep.

"Bishop." Tyrell Suggs said, standing over him.

Larry had accidentally fallen off in the second guest bedroom.

Now as he opened his eyes—it taking him a moment to realize where he was—he saw his friend in the faint light from the hallway that came in the partially open door.

"Yeah, wha...what is it?" Larry said.

"It's done."

Larry questioned Tyrell Suggs with a look, although he believed he knew what the man was referring to.

He had wanted to go, witness the younger Bonner's death, wanted to be the one that pulled the trigger, but Tyrell Suggs fought him on that. He told Larry it didn't matter how much he wanted to be there, he just couldn't let him commit the act. But Tyrell Suggs knew of someone who would do the crime, who had obviously just done it.

"Really?" Larry said, slowly sitting up, throwing his legs over the edge of the bed. "He's sure?"

"Got the call a couple minutes ago. He sent me a few cell phone pictures for proof. You wanna see them?"

"No, no," Larry waved Tyrell Suggs off, the image of the dead Bonner lying bloody, his brains on the pavement, just as Larry had seen in his dreams, would've been more than Larry needed to see. "If your guy says the job is done, that's good enough for me."

27

Bright fluorescent lights hung over him as Paul walked down a hallway behind a man wearing a white lab coat, white pants and tennis shoes.

"Are you Paul Taylor?" the man said moments ago, stepping out from behind a heavy steal door with a tiny square window. Paul had been sitting alone, impatiently for almost twenty minutes in a small waiting room with only three chairs.

"Yeah," Paul said, trying to suppress the fear he felt, trying not to let it come out in his voice.

"I need to see some ID," the man said, never meeting Paul's eyes, but looking just over his shoulder.

"Yeah, okay," Paul said, pulling his wallet from his back pocket, fingering out his driver's license. The man took it, slid it under the clip on his board, jotting down information before handing it back.

After seeing the video of the horrible things done to his daughter, Paul raced out the house, vowing to find Bishop Larry Lakes, come as close as possible to beating the man to death with his fists, then drag him barely breathing to the police, payment for whatever he did to get his daughter in that room with those boys.

But Paul needed to talk to his daughter first, find out exactly what happened.

Pushing the Dodge much faster than he should've been going, his phone pressed to his ear, Paul cursed as yet again, his call to Shayla went straight to voicemail.

"Fuck!" He threw the phone down, took a hard turn, leading him to the street where the rehabilitation center stood.

Shayla would be there, Paul told himself, praying that would be the case. The reception person would call her room, she'd come down, eyes averted, ashamed of what she had done. He would open his arms, hug her tight, and when she told him she had used again, that it was the drug that made her do those things, and that she would never do anything like that again, Paul would hold her tighter, kiss her head, tell her that he forgave her, that he loved her, and she would always be his little girl.

But that didn't happen.

When Paul pulled up to the center, there was a police car sitting curbside, blue lights flashing, a single officer leaning against the cruiser, looking as though he had much more important places to be than there.

Paul walked toward the building doors. One of the doors was propped open, and inside Paul could see there was another uniformed officer speaking to one of the center's employees.

"What's happening in there?" Paul asked the cop standing by his car.

He was a large white man with big forearms and black knuckle-out leather gloves on his hands. A radio clipped to his chest chattered about crimes being committed about Atlanta.

"Dead body was found here couple hours ago," the officer said with little interest.

Paul felt his knees would give when he heard this news, but told himself it wasn't his daughter the officer spoke of. It wasn't Shayla. "A guy?"

"Naw." The cop looked down the street, then turned looking the opposite way, around Paul. "Female, black, around nineteen or twenty. Drug overdose. Fucking shame."

"Where is she?" Paul said feeling his pulse race.

"Excuse me?" The officer said, eyeing Paul for the first time.

"Is she in there?" Paul said, his voice high pitched. He turned, pointing toward the building. "Is she?"

"Sir, is there a problem?" The officer said, setting a leather gloved hand on Paul's shoulder.

Paul felt light headed, felt the street, the buildings around him slowly start to whirl. "I need to know the girl's name."

"We can't tell you that, sir, till we reach her next of—"

"I might be her next of kin," Paul said, frantically grabbing the office by the arm. "I think that girl is my daughter! I need to know where she is."

The man wearing the white lab coat stopped in front of another heavy steal door, another small glass square at the top end of it. He waited for Paul to step in front of it, then the man pulled it open.

"After you, sir," he said.

Paul stepped inside the room—white, square tiles on the walls, bigger ones on the floor. He noticed a drain in the center of the floor, stainless steal sinks against one wall of the room, and big steal freezer doors on the other.

"Step all the way in sir," the jacketed man told him, and only then did Paul realize he was standing statue like in the doorway, afraid to take a step inside.

Two tables with locked wheels on the feet stood in the center of the room. One was empty, a flat metal surface, rows and rows of tiny holes in it. The other table...there was a body on it, covered with a white sheet.

Paul wanted to turn. He wanted to run. He was coated in cold sweat, his stomach churned queasily, a voice inside of him began to pray.

For privacy reasons, the police said they could not give the name of the girl they had found until family had been identified, but since he claimed to be her father, they would allow him to see her.

Standing over whoever's poor child this was, Paul continued silently praying.

Please, please God. Don't let this be my child on this table. I hadn't done right by her, but You gave me another chance, don't take that from me now. Please!

The man dressed in white stood at the head of the table, a corner of the sheet in his hand. He asked if Paul he was ready.

His eyes still close, Paul bargained with God, promised to give his life whenever He was ready to take it—in ten years or ten minutes—if He just made it that Shayla wasn't the girl lying before him.

"Sir," the man said, pulling Paul out of his thoughts.

He opened his eyes, cleared his throat and steadied himself. "I'm ready."

"Take your time. There's no rush."

Paul nodded.

The man pulled back the sheet, lowered it to just below the young woman's collar bones. He stepped back, out of the way somewhere, leaving Paul to determine whether or not the girl that lay on the metal slab was the one he allowed to fall into a life of drug addiction, homelessness and possible prostitution.

Paul stood staring down, eyes locked on the face of the woman, attempting to change what he saw before him. He tried to alter the shape of the young woman's nose, lower her cheekbones, thin out her lips, so that the girl lying dead there didn't so closely resemble him.

He dropped a hand to the table, steadying himself, for his knees did buckle that time. Paul smeared the tears that raced down his cheeks, looked over his shoulder, locating the man off in a corner of the room, nodded at him, smearing his hand over his face again.

"Sir? Is that—" the man started, hurrying over.

"Yes," Paul said, mournfully. "This is my daughter."

28

Larry didn't know how long it would take for police to find Officer Bonner's killer, but reports of his death were already on every news channel.

This morning on TV, Larry saw a crowd of reporters running behind Mayor Bonner, chasing him with microphones and cell phone recorders, bombarding him with questions. The big man turned to face them, surrounded by his aids and other drones, Bonner looked devastated, lost and heartbroken, as though someone had just then whispered the news of his son's death.

"If you would please respect our right to privacy during this horrible period, we'd—"

Larry paused the TV, staring satisfied at the look of gut wrenching grief on the mayor's face. Larry imagined the mayor's wife at home, locked in a dark room, curtains drawn, tears streaming down her face, howling, mourning the death of their son.

Maybe it would come back to him, Larry thought, now standing outside the gate of his son's school. Maybe after really thinking about it, Bonner's fat ass would put two and two together, recall some of the conversations he had with Larry, Larry's warnings not to come after him or there would be an insurmountable price to pay. Maybe the mayor was talking to the police that very moment, telling them to go looking for Larry, to bring him in for questioning.

But Larry hadn't time for that.

Larry had been thinking about his own son.

He drove over to the school, parked the car and waited for the children to be let out for recess.

When the doors opened, scores of children rushed out at the sound of the bell, gleeful, high-pitched screams proceeding them.

Stepping closer to the fence, poking his fingers through the chain link, his face so close it almost touched metal, Larry looked for his son.

He heard the boy's voice first, then saw Jabari chasing a child across the playground, laughing.

He felt a pang of disappointment, expecting Jabari to be overwrought with despair, his head lowered, moping about by himself, distraught by the fact he had not seen his father in weeks. Maybe his mother told him Larry was on a business trip, that everything was fine, and there was no need to worry.

"Jabari!" Larry called out when his son was close enough to hear him.

Jabari stopped running, looked around for whoever was calling him, then spotting his father, he froze, looking dumbfounded by what his next move would be—like his mother might've told him if ever in this position, run away.

"Jabari! Come over here!" Larry said.

Jabari walked over, uncertainty in each step. He stopped in front of his father, stared up at him through the fence. "Dad?"

"Son, how are you?" Larry smiled, admiring how handsome his boy looked. It appeared he had grown an inch or so in the short time Larry had been away. "How you been?"

"What's going on, Dad?"

Larry could tell by the concern in the question that his son did care, that he was troubled by his father's absence.

"Let's hang out," Larry said, smiling. "We can go somewhere and talk, get a couple of cheeseburgers like we used to. You wanna do that?"

Jabari threw a glance over his shoulder, then turned back to Larry. "But what about school?"

"School will be here. We can sign you out early. Don't you wanna hang with your Dad? We can do whatever you want. Whatever you wanna do. I promise."

The worry on the boy's face gave way to excitement and a smile. "Okay."

Jabari wanted cheeseburgers as Larry promised him.

They sat in a booth at the closest McDonald's. The boy talked about school, projects he was assigned, the video game he was playing at home — waving his hands about in front of his face, trying to explain the concept of the game's story.

Larry would let the boy have his fun, not torment him with questions about what was going on back at the house. He would let his son enjoy the cheeseburgers and fries he asked for. They'd catch a matinee, and Larry would pretend as though nothing bad was happening, that things hadn't changed one bit.

In the darkened movie theater, Larry watched his son's face, lit by the animation of some superhero on the screen, punching his way through a mob of vicious alien monsters.

Jabari jumped in his seat, yelled, laughed and turned to Larry every time there was an explosion, and said, "Ooh, Dad! Did you see that?"

After the movie, Larry checked him and Jabari into a hotel room.

He spared no expense, putting them in the Buckhead Ritz Carlton, right across the street from where they had seen the movie.

Inside, they sat in the sitting room of the suite Larry had gotten them, the TV on, airing cartoons, the volume just loud enough for Jabari to hear.

Larry stared at his phone, the screen flashing, silently ringing on mute, Marian's number blinking. No doubt, she or Paul had gone to pick up Jabari, was told that Larry had taken him out early, and now the woman was probably losing her mind, wondering exactly what he might do to their son. Larry resented that she would allow Paul, almost a stranger, to spend time alone with Jabari, but was frightened at the very thought of Larry doing the same. Exactly what did she think he would do? What did she believe him capable of?

Larry reached across the sofa, rubbed Jabari's head and smiled. If Marian knew how much he loved his son, she would know that the child was never safer than when he was with his father.

He waited for the phone to stop flashing then pulled up the text screen. He thumbed a message and sent it to his wife.

Jabari is fine. I have him. Don't worry.

Not thirty seconds later, he received a response.

BRING HIM HOME NOW! I'LL CALL THE POLICE!!!

Larry could hear Marian screaming the threat at him with all the exclamation points at the end. He wasn't concerned. She could call the police if she wanted. Jabari was still his son.

I'll bring him back when I feel like it!

After sending the message, Larry powered down his phone, set it on the end
table beside the sofa, grabbed the remote from the coffee table and muted
the TV.

"Now tell me what's going on at home," Larry said.

"What do you mean, Dad?" Jabari said, looking at him as though
wondering why he had to turn down the TV in order to ask that question.

"How is your sister?"

"She's fine. She's supposed to go on a field trip to the zoo tomorrow,
and—"

"That's good," Larry said, cutting Jabari off, wanting to get to what
interested him. "How is your mother doing?"

Jabari looked uncomfortable, as though maybe his mother told the boy
not to tell his father anything if he asked. "She's fine."

"Have you heard anything about her marrying Paul? Is that really
supposed to happen?"

"I...I guess." Jabari averted his eyes.

"Look at me when I'm talking to you," Larry demanded. "Have you
heard about Paul proposing to your mother or not?" Larry said, feeling
himself becoming jealous. It was something he did not want his boy to see.
It was sign of weakness, he knew that, and forced himself to calm some. He
softened his stare and readdressed his son. "You don't have anything to
worry about. Did they tell you about this or not?"

Jabari nodded, looking as though he knew he was telling his father exactly what he did not want to hear. "Mom didn't, but he did."

Larry envisioned Paul pulling Jabari aside, stooping down in front of him in a hallway, letting him know he was going to ask for his mother's hand in marriage, and what did the boy think about it. It was the answer to the question Larry wanted to know that moment.

"Do you like that idea?" Larry asked. "Your mother marrying Paul?"

"There's no way that you and Mom can get back together?" Jabari asked.

Marian had let Larry know that she had spoken to the kids, told them of their breakup, their impending divorce, the fact that they wouldn't be seeing a lot of their father anymore. The children took it hard, Marian told him. There was a lot of crying. Larry stood on the other end of the phone when she gave him that news, seething, resenting Marian for not allowing Larry to be included in breaking the news to them.

"We aren't getting back together, son," Larry told Jabari.

The boy nodded, his face stern, as if trying to take the news like a man, the way he knew his father would've wanted him to.

"I guess it won't be that bad having Paul there," Jabari said, sounding upbeat. "It looks like he makes Mom happy, and it'll kinda be like having two dads."

Tightening his grip on the arm of the sofa, his muscles contracting as if from physical pain, Larry knew he couldn't have heard his son correctly. He believed the boy said something about seeing another man as his father, considering Paul in the way he would consider Larry, as the though that man had sacrificed as Larry had all these years, as though Paul would've given his life for the boy, would've risked his own life, because he was the man that brought Jabari into this world, even though it was not him, but Larry. He knew he hadn't heard Jabari correctly, but found himself standing over his son, wanting to reach down, yank him up by his collar, shake sense into him.

"What did you just say?"

"I...I—"

"You see that man as a father to you?" Larry said, his voice raised.

Jabari stammered, shaking his head, but unable to speak.

"Answer me, boy!"

"He...I—"

Before he could speak another word, Larry had slapped the child hard across the face, sending the boy's glasses flying from his eyes to the carpet—Jabari toppling over after them.

Moments later, inside the hotel bathroom, Larry pulled the syringe from his arm, sitting it on the toilet lid, his head thrown back, his legs kicked out in front of him. He winced in troubled ecstasy as the drug swam up the river of veins in his arm.

He needed the escape, to quickly pull away. He hadn't meant to beat the boy like that, he just wasn't prepared for the shock of Jabari's admission.

Now Larry pulled himself to his feet, wobbled a bit, told himself he would make the lapse in judgment up to his son. He was sure Jabari knew his father loved him, but maybe he didn't know just how much. Maybe, since Larry hadn't seen the boy in a while, Jabari had forgotten.

Larry pulled back the shower curtain, reached in, turning both knobs, running the water, checking the temperature with his fingers until it was warm. He didn't want to scald the boy's delicates skin.

Standing in the mirror again, he unbuttoned his shirt, peeled it off then pulled his t-shirt up over his head, leaving his chest bare.

He opened the bathroom door, stepped out into the sitting room, saw that his son's face was still buried in the sofa pillow. He had stopped the crying he had been doing, the crying that forced Larry into the bathroom just after he had hit the boy.

Larry stepped closer to the sofa, stood just over his son. "You know I love you, don't you?"

Jabari turned, looked up at his father with bloodshot eyes, surprised to see his Dad semi-nude.

"Did you hear me, son? You know I love you, don't you?"

Jabari nodded, then quickly answered, "Yes," as if remembering the lesson just taught him for not speaking up.

"Do you love me?" Larry asked.

"Yeah, Dad. I love you."

Larry smiled, extended an open hand to him.

Jabari reached out, took it, apprehension in the gesture, hesitation on his face, as if taking the hand of a stranger.

Larry pulled his boy off the sofa.

"Where are we going?"

"Don't worry, you'll see," Larry said, leading Jabari toward the bathroom.

29

Marian stood, Simone standing beside her, in the front student office of Jabari's school, wanting to strangle the schoolteacher who told her she had released Jabari into his father's custody.

"What do you mean he left with his father? You let him go?" Marian shrieked, craning her neck, looking up and down the hallway, as if the middle-aged woman couldn't have possibly been telling the truth.

"Bishop Lakes came to get him and I let him go. What…what did I do wrong?"

Marian stared so angrily at the woman — contemplating the danger she might have put her child in — that she couldn't form words. "If my child gets hurt…you'll pay for this. I swear to God."

She dragged Simone by the hand out to the truck, opened the door, hoisted her up into the back seat by the arm.

"Wait right here! I have a call to make," Marian said, one arm sunk into her purse, digging out her cell phone. She slammed the truck door closed, paced away from the Lexus, the phone to ear, cursing her husband under her breath as it rang. Larry never picked up.

After going home and pacing the kitchen for hours, looking up at the clock every few minutes, the cellphone she clutched in her sweaty grip finally rang. It was a call from the front gate.

"Hello? Hello!" Marian said, breathless.

"It's me," Larry said, something sounding not quite right about his voice. "Come get your son."

Marian stabbed the keys to remotely open the gate and ran to the front door, threw it open, hurried out the house, across the front lawn, intending to rip Larry to shreds for taking Jabari. But as Marian slowed to a halt just feet in front of her son, Larry's car was nowhere in sight. All Marian saw was a beat up Toyota Corolla speeding away. She continued over to Jabari, sensing something was wrong. He looked odd, frightened for some reason. She kneeled in front of him, grabbed him, pulled him into her, hugging him tight, as if someone just rescued him from a burning building, one that she was certain had taken her child.

"Was that your father?" Marian asked, holding Jabari at arm's length.

Jabari said nothing. He stared at his mother, slack-jawed and glaze-eyed, as though frozen, his mind stuck on a memory he could not pull away from.

"Jabari!" Marian shook him. His head rolled about on his neck, his body feeling so limp in her arms, she was surprised he was able to hold himself up. "Jabari, what's wrong with you? Are you all right? Talk to me?" She shook him again, harder this time until she saw his eyes focus on her. "Are you okay?"

"I'm fine."

"No, Jabari you aren't. I can see...did he...did he..." Marian feared asking the question, frightened of the answer. "...did he touch you?"

Looking her in the eyes, Marian thought she saw resentment in his stare, blame for allowing him to be taken, and wonder at how she could ask such a question when she already knew the answer.

A tear spilled from his eye, ran down his cheek. He lowered his head in shame, looked back up at Marian a second later then shook his head.

Marian stared disbelievingly at him. He said that Larry hadn't done anything to him, but the expression of pain, guilt and shame on his face said something entirely different. The poor boy was lying for his father, not wanting him to get him trouble.

She grabbed him even tighter still, looked him deep into his eyes, feeling tears trying to fall from her own, but she held them back, needing to appear strong in front of him.

"You can tell me, Jabari. Please, you can tell me. Did your father put a hand on you? Did he do anything at all that made you uncomfortable, anything that you felt he shouldn't have done?"

Sadness in his eyes, an expression she had never seen on his face before, Jabari shook his head, and as if rehearsed, without any emotion at all said, "No, Mom. Dad did nothing to me."

30

"I wanna take you out for the day. Take you to the park, or for a movie. Would you like that?" Larry told his father, Lincoln.

He had felt the need to go back and visit the man in the nursing home.

"Why?" Lincoln said, skeptical.

"Because I never do. It's my fault you're left in here all by yourself. I'm going to do better by you," Larry said, grabbing the remote from the nightstand beside the bed. He turned off the TV, took his father's arm and helped him up from the chair.

"Do they know you're taking me?" Lincoln asked.

"I told the people at the front when I came in. But when we leave, I'll sign you out so they'll know, Dad."

Larry helped his father into his jacket, one arm carefully through the sleeve then the other. He started to walk his father toward the door.

"My hat," Lincoln said, turning toward the closet.

"I got it, Dad," Larry said, going back, reaching up on the top shelf, grabbing Lincoln's driving cap and setting it atop his father's head.

"Where are we?" Lincoln asked, not half an hour later. He stared out the windshield of the old Toyota, searching for a sign on the hotel.

An attendant dressed in a slacks and a vest, pulled open his door.

"We have to make a stop, Dad," Larry said, pushing open his door.

"I thought you said you were taking me to lunch."

"I just wanna make this stop. We're going to go up to the room for just a moment, okay."

Larry and his father stood in the elevator alone, staring at the door as the carriage lifted them to the tenth floor. Out the corner of his eye, Larry glanced at his father, the man who used to be healthy and strong and demanding was now weak, shriveled and soft spoken. To Larry, he hardly looked like the same man at all, and Larry had to work harder than he wanted to still associate Lincoln with the horrible things he had done to him as a child. It had been more than thirty years since his father set a hand on him—longer than that since he had arranged for other men to abuse him. But that wasn't because Lincoln saw the error of his ways. The man had never apologized, had never recognized himself as being wrong.

A "ding" sounded as the elevator doors opened. Larry helped his father off.

"This way Dad," Larry said, walking just in front of Lincoln, leading him down the hallway toward his hotel room.

"I'm hungry," Lincoln complained. "You said we were going to lunch and—"

"We will, Dad," Larry said, slipping the key card into the reader, opening the door, thinking about the last time his father had abused him so many years ago Lincoln had stumbled in one night from drinking, smelling of liquor, pissed the fuck off about something, mumbling his hatred for the life he had to endure. Larry was making a sandwich in the kitchen during a commercial break of a show he was watching. Lincoln marched through the living room, and didn't speak a word as he stormed into the kitchen, grabbing Larry, throwing him against the counter, holding his head down against the cold counter, as he yanked down his son's pants and took him more brutally than he ever had.

Just after that, after Lincoln snatched up his slacks, and disappeared as quickly as he had appeared, Larry stood in the bathroom, angrily staring down at the blood that stained the clump of tissue he had just wiped himself with. He glared at himself in the mirror, pants around his knees, t-shirt hiked up to his chest, scars and scrapes on his face from the many tussles he and his father had.

Larry told himself that would be the last time. He would die before his father did that to him again, and Larry readied himself for the next time. But it never came. There just seemed a loss of interest on Lincoln's part.

Nights, lying in bed after that, Larry's heart would thumping in his chest, hearing his father walk in the apartment slamming the door, Larry would reach under the mattress, feel for the carving knife he had stashed there. But Lincoln would not enter Larry's room.

After months without incident, Larry realized that it was over — the torture, the terror, the panicking and punishment — it was all over. He was overjoyed, but believed he was somewhat saddened as well, never being able to take out the resentment he had against his father for the years of abuse.

"Son! Did you hear what I said?"

Lincoln's voice jarred Larry out of his thoughts. In that voice was the tone his father used all those years ago, when he had complete control over Larry, when Larry was a helpless boy, and could do nothing to defend himself.

"I'm sorry, Dad," Larry said, politely to his father, who sat in the same place Jabari had when Larry pulled him off the sofa, and took him into the bathroom.

An image flashed across Larry's mind.

He shut his eyes, but it had already imprinted itself in his head—the hot shower steam, the water crashing against his son's narrow back, the boy struggling, his body wet and soap-slippery in Larry's grasp--Jabari's shrill cry, the begging, and Larry telling him, as Lincoln had told Larry so many times, "It'll be okay. It'll be fine." Then trying to quiet him. "Shh, shh, shh!" And as he held tight to the boy, his back hunched over Jabari's, Larry yelling over his son's suffering—"I love you, son! It's only because I love you!"

His vision clouded, he wiped at his cheek, then looked up at his father, who was staring at him oddly.

"Why you crying, boy?" Lincoln asked.

Larry touched his face, looked down at his fingertips to see that they were wet. He wiped the tears on his shirt. "I'm mourning the loss of my childhood."

"What? What are you talking about?"

"You never apologized for what you did to me. You never apologized, Dad."

"Larry—"

"So I'm crying for that frightened boy that you say you loved, but cared not a damn thing about."

"Son, I did love you! I do!"

"And I'm crying for the monster you made that boy become," Larry said, ignoring his father's declaration.

Lincoln shifted back a little on the cushions, questioning his son's remark.

Larry scooted closer to his father, their knees almost touching, and very softly, looking intently into his father's aging eyes, he said, "You've made me the monster you are. God have mercy on our souls."

Larry leaned forward, clamping one, then the other hand around his father's throat and began to squeeze.

Eyes bulging, Lincoln grabbed Larry's wrists, trying to pry his son's hands from around his neck.

Larry felt his father struggling, writhing beneath him, he knew he would not be strong enough to break Larry's grip.

"Son! Son, please!" Lincoln coughed, his mouth open wide.

Larry ignored the old man's pleads, lifting himself up, kneeling on the cushions over his father, pressing all of his weight down on Lincoln's throat. He felt the man's airway collapse and Larry pressed harder, tears spilling from both men's eyes. With everything he had, all his might, Larry continued to violently strangle his father. Feeling the man kick him in the legs, scratch his arms, draw blood, Larry was outside of himself again, floating somewhere high in the corner of the room, staring down at his arched back, his muscular arms pulling the old man in by the throat, slamming his head back against the spine of the sofa, yelling, "I hate you! Just die! Why don't you just fucking die?" And after another eternity of his father fighting for life, beating on Larry's arms—hard at first, then softer and softer, till Lincoln's arms dropped to his sides and Lincoln gasped futilely for the air Larry deprived him of—after all that, Lincoln's body went limp, Larry almost feeling his father's spirit rise out of him.

Exhausted, Larry fell over, his head dropping into his father's lap. His chest heaving, he gasped heavily, wrapping his arms around Lincoln's waist, holding the dead man tight, as he sobbed loudly and uncontrollably.

31

There was nowhere else he could go, nowhere else where he would be accepted, nowhere else he wanted to be, so Larry was not surprised when he looked up—not even realizing when he turned corners and proceeded through green lights—that he was parked in front of the mansion, the place he had called home for the most recent part of his tortured life.

Marian would not want to see him. She would still be angry for him spending time with his own son, but she had no right. Larry would make her understand that when he explained why they should be a family again.

He was sure Jabari hadn't spoke a word to his mother about the loving experience he had shared with his father. It had been a little rough on the boy, probably more traumatizing than Larry had thought it would've been, but figured, next time it would be easier for Jabari.

Larry looked up at the house as he balanced on the side of his fist a pinch of heroin he had taken from the zipper bag he kept in the dash. He had already come down from what he had used earlier in the hotel bathroom and sensed he needed to get his head right to deal with whatever situation Marian would present him with.

He lifted his fist to his nose, quickly inhaled the small amount of crushed drug and allowed it to do its work. His muscles tightened, his eyes widened as he was jerked back into the car seat. His mouth wrenched open, his body convulsed momentarily, then settled, his lids falling low, his head slumping forward. He sat there, deathly still for a second, then shook his head wildly, as if to clear it of cobwebs.

Larry wiped a tear from the corner of his eye, looked to the mansion and wondered if the man would be there—If Paul had saw the video yet of his daughter, Shayla—and if he had learned his lesson to leave Larry's family alone. Larry was sure he probably had. He would be fighting angry, possibly killing angry, as Larry would've been if some man had done the same thing to Simone.

So Larry turned in his seat, looked around the car for something to beat the man down with if it came to that.

32

It was as though hell rose to visit them on earth, Marian thought as she banged on Jabari's door. After he had yelled at her, told her that Larry had not lay a finger on him, he hurried into the house, ran upstairs and locked himself into his room.

Marian hurried behind him, for she hadn't believed—despite how much she wanted—that the boy had not been assaulted. She knew her child, knew when he was hurt, when he was mentally anguished and scared. Jabari appeared to have been all those things when she held him in front of her outside on the front lawn.

She banged on his door, over and over again, but no matter how many times, how she demanded and pleaded that he open it, he would not.

Marian went down stairs, spent the next two hours attempting to get Larry on his phone, find out exactly what happened, but was unable get him. She tried Paul after that, but was unable to get him either.

Finally, she thought to call the police, but heard the front door open then close so hard it practically rattled the entire foundation of the mansion.

"Marian! Marian, are you here?"

"In here!" She started out of the kitchen, running into Paul.

His chest heaving, his face shiny with sweat, looking as though the world had just come to an end, he took her tight by her shoulders.

"What's wrong?" Marian said.

"They found my daughter," Paul said, taking two steps toward her. "She 's dead."

"I'm sorry, Paul. I'm so sorry." She went to him, hugged him. "We need to call the police. Tell them Larry had something to do with it."

"How can we prove that?"

"The DVD."

"I broke it, remember. There is no proof, and there's nothing they're gonna do," Paul said, pulling away from Marian.

"You don't know that."

"A 19 year-old girl—a black girl, addicted to drugs, dies in the hood. How many times does that happen? And how many times has nothing been done about it?"

Far too many times, Marian thought, believing it was rhetorical question, not requiring a question. But Paul yelled, hammering a fist down on the table.

"How many, Marian?"

"Too many," Marian coughed the answer up, startled, then watched Paul pace three quick lines the length of the kitchen. She knew he was plotting his next move, and when he stopped, turned to her, she could see on his face that the deliberation was over—he had come to a decision and she feared she knew what it was.

"Paul, no." Marian shook her head.

"The police aren't gonna do a damn thing, but my baby's not gonna die in vain." He started toward the hallway that led to the front door.

"Where are you going?" Marian asked, chasing behind him.

"To find your husband. I have to find him," Paul said, yanking open the front door, running out of it.

33

Larry had left the car outside the gate, the trunk open, after pulling the tire iron from it. He had tossed the tool through the bars of the fence, picked it back up after climbing the gate and throwing himself over.

His head still spinning, it feeling almost detached from his body, he stood on the front porch, wondering exactly how he would get in the house. Would he try to go around back, check for open windows, or would he ring the bell and hope that he was let in?

Surprised, he saw that he didn't have to deal with any of that, for the front door flew open, and to his shock, Paul stood in front of him, breathing heavily, appearing as astonished as Larry.

Without thinking, Larry wielded the tire iron, catching the momentarily stunned man on the side of his head. Paul's skin split open, blood spilling from the wound as he staggered about, pin-balling off the hallway walls, back toward the kitchen, before dropping to the floor.

Larry hadn't noticed his wife till he heard her screaming. He looked up to see Marian, her hands to her face, screaming as though Larry had actually murdered Paul. She was about to lower herself to Paul's body, sprawled out on the floor, when Larry stepped over him, snatched Marian by the hair, yanking her up. She screamed louder, as though Larry was going to hurt her again.

"Let me go! Get your hands off of me!"

The noise coming from her was deafening, so much that Larry struck her again, hoping that she would quiet down. It only served to make her cry out louder. Knowing nothing else to do, Larry let go of her hair, spun her around to face him, grabbing by her by the front of her shirt and shaking her.

"Shhhh, shhhh!" Larry tried to quiet her. She continued to cry, her eyes focused on the floor, where Paul had fallen.

Larry glanced in that direction, saw Paul was bleeding profusely from the head, Larry thinking there was a chance he might die from the wound.

"Look at me," Larry said, shaking Marian. "Look at me!"

Her eyes landed on him; they were wide and unblinking.

"Good," Larry said. "I don't want to hurt you. Do you hear me?"

Marian nodded, appeared frightened for her life. Larry could feel her trembling in his grip.

"I need for you to say it. I need for you to say you understand me," Larry said.

"I…I understand," Marian whimpered, the tears still coming steadily down her face.

"Good, now tell me where my children are. They here?"

Marian shook her head. "No…they aren't here."

"Don't lie to me, Marian. Are they here."

"No!" She screamed, seeming fed of being held. She grabbed for Larry's wrists, dug her fingernails into them, gouging deep scars into them, causing Larry to pull back. He gasped at the blood that spilled freely from the wounds his father had opened, reared back, and struck his wife hard across the face with the back of his hand.

She spun, arms whipping round, plummeting to the ground. She hit the floor, and Larry was on top of her, grabbing her again by the hair atop her head.

34

Lying on his stomach, Jabari was in agony; his lower half felt on fire. Why had his father done that to him? Why did he hurt him that way.

Steam so thick Jabari could hardly see in the shower—the water so hot, it scalded his skin, but that pain was nothing compared to what his father did to him. It felt as though his insides were being ripped out from inside of him.

Jabari tried to fight him—tried to throw punches behind him—tried to free himself from his father's grasp. But his father was huge—much stronger than him. The floor of the tub was slippery with water and soap, rendering Jabari defenseless against the attack. He shut his eyes, tightened his arms across his body, clenched every muscle and screamed until he thought he would black out. Sadly he didn't. He was conscious, wide awake for every moment of the hell his father unleashed on him, until his father yelled out, gripping Jabari even tighter, almost pushing them both into the front wall of the shower. Then moments later, Jabari felt his father convulsing behind him, felt something spilling inside of him, and then he was released.

On the ride back to the house, Jabari shivered against the horrifying thought of his father pulling the car to the curb on some deserted street, under some dark overpass, reaching over and abusing him again.

His father apologized the entire ride home, telling him he only did what he did because he loved him.

"Do you believe me?" His farther asked.

Jabari continued to stare out the window, wishing his father would drive faster so that he could just be out of his site.

"Do you believe me son?" His father asked more forcefully, reaching over, touching Jabari's knee, causing Jabari to retract, throw himself against the door, consider jumping out of the moving car.

When he got home, when his mother grabbed him by the shoulders, stared in his face, asked him that question, he knew she was fully aware of what had happened, but still he couldn't tell her. He didn't know why, but he couldn't admit to it. All he wanted to be was left alone.

Thankfully, she had let him go, allowed him to lock himself in his room, sort out his thoughts. But she came back, banging on the door, and still he could not face her, for he knew what had happened to him was his fault and no one else's.

Now, still sobbing, thinking he would never be able to stop, Jabari thought he had heard something. He lifted his head from the pillow, looked around, listened harder and realized he had heard screams.

He sat up in bed, thinking that it had sounded like his mother's voice. Thinking it might have been his imagination, he was about lie down again, when he heard another cry accompanied by yelling. This voice sounded like his father's.

Frightened, Jabari threw his legs over the side of the bed, hurried to his door, wrapped a hand around the knob, reluctant to turn it, fearing his father was waiting just outside. But the screaming and yelling continued, assuring him that his father was still down stairs, sounding as though he was doing something terrible to his mother.

He opened the door, the screams amplified, curdling his blood, making him cry, making him think his father was doing to his mother, what he had did to him in the hotel.

He stepped out of the room, cautiously down the hall, knowing that he had to help his mother. Halting just outsider her closed door, he knew what he had to do.

Inside his mother's bedroom, Jabari looked around for something to stand on. Spotting the ottoman, he grabbed it from in front of the corner chair, pushed it toward the closet, and after opening the closet door, he slid the ottoman just inside, stepping on top of it.

Blindly, he reached an arm up onto the top shelf. Breathing heavily, his mother's gut wrenching cries still assaulting his ears, he felt the gun he had found two days ago while playing in his mother's room—the gun he was told never to touch.

Larry would kill her, Marian thought, as she felt him grab her again by the hair and yank her off the floor after he had struck her across the face with the back of his hand.

The pain had been so extreme, so exquisite, she was on the very edge of blacking out, but knew if she had, that would free him to search the house for Jabair, and Simone; he would take them and never bring them back to her, and there was no telling what he'd do with them.

"Take me to them!" Larry said. "I know they're here," Larry wrenched Marian's head back, yelling in her ear.

Still holding her by the hair, he forced her around in the direction of the stairs, but Marian fought him, reached behind her and grabbed at his wrists again, feeling the sticky warm blood she had drawn when she cut him moments ago.

"No!" Marian screamed. "They're aren't here! No!"

With his other hand, Larry grabbed Marian around the throat, tossed her about to face the stairs.

She gasped with surprised, horrified to find Jabair standing in front of them, his arm outstretched and trembling, her gun in his hand.

"Jabari...baby..." Marian started. There was something in his eyes, not just fear like before, but anger, something hateful and murderous, and that moment, despite what her son had told her—that moment when she witnessed how Jabari looked at his father—she knew that the man had did something horrible to her son.

"Baby, don't," Marians said, frightened he'd do something he'd forever regret.

Marian felt Larry's grip on her loosen—he let her go entirely. She thought to step in front of him, shield him, protect Larry—the man she once loved—place herself between him and her son, attempt to say something to calm Jabari, but Larry threw her aside, telling her that he could speak to his own son.

He stood in front of the boy, slowly raising his hands to shoulder height. He shook his head as though conveying a message to his son that what the boy was doing was wrong.

"Put down the gun, son," Larry said. "You know you don't want to do this."

Jabari swallowed hard, blinked his eyes several times.

"Jabari, we can talk about this. Why don't you..." Larry continued, taking a step forward.

But before he could speak a word, Jabari shut his eyes, squeezed the trigger of the gun and fired off three shots.

The fire flash from the gun was blinding, the "pops" deafening, forcing Marin to close her eyes, cover her ears and drop to her knees for fear of getting shot herself.

She heard the undeniable sound of a body hitting the floor and she knew Larry had fallen. Jabari's cries, even louder than the gunfire, filled the room, making Marin press her hands harder against her ears. As she kneeled, she dared to open an eye,
look to her left. She saw her husband, blood spilling from his open mouth, gazing lifelessly at her, his hand reaching out, as if to be saved. And then she

saw Jabari, stepping in between his father's splayed legs, firing the last of the bullets, point blank into his Larry's chest.

EPILOGUE

Exactly one year to do the day, the sun shown and warmed their faces as they stood in the cemetery and gazed down at the headstone reading "Father, Husband, Son". Below that was his name, "Larry Leonard Lakes"—his date of birth, homecoming date, and nothing else.

Surprisingly, it was Jabari's idea to come.

He had been in therapy since the shooting, and over the year, he had progressed a great deal, no longer locking himself up in his room, or "closing himself off" mentally, even when sitting at dinner with the family, or at school, in a room full of kids.

"Are you sure that's something you want to do?" Marian sat down in front of him and asked when he brought up the idea a week ago.

Jabari took a moment, as if to look inside his memory, compare the father he knew most of his life to the father that had abused him. Jabari nodded. "I don't think I'll ever want to go again, but this time I think we should. This can be the only time."

Standing there at the grave, watching as her son lay a bouquet of flowers at his father's headstone, Marian was so proud of him, considering how conflicted he must've been.

Jabari had loved his father. Even on the day he took his father's life, just after the boy fired the last bullet, he threw the gun aside, fell to Larry's chest, demanding that he wake up. It took all Marian's strength to pull the boy away, realizing that her son's only intention was to hurt his father for what he had done to Jabari, not kill him.

Thankfully, Simone had not seen Larry die, but she did come running down the stairs crying when she heard the shooting, and when she stumbled into kitchen, saw Larry, Jabari pulling at his father's shirt, covered with the man's blood, and Paul lying on the floor in a mess of his own blood, Simone screamed then fainted.

The police, fire department, Emory paramedics and the medical examiner all converged on the house not half an hour after the incident.

Larry's body was taken away. Paul was taken to the emergency room, while Marian stayed at home, needing to answer questions from police and detectives on the scene.

When Marian visited Paul the next day (the awful gash in his head was stitched up and he was kept overnight for the concussion he suffered) he lay in bed, his head bandaged, looking at Marian as though he had failed her.

"I'm so sorry," Paul said, reaching out an IV punctured hand for Marian. "I was helpless. He hit me, and all I could do was watch what was happening from the floor, and pray he didn't—"

"Stop it," Marian said, sitting beside him, comforting him, kissing his face. "It's over. There was nothing more you could've done. It's over and we're all fine."

"Even Jabari?"

"He will be," Marian said, raising Paul's hand to her lips, kissing the back of it. "We'll find him the best therapist and he will be fine. So you just worry about getting better, and—"

"I'm not leaving," Paul interrupted.

"Not leaving where?"

"Not leaving your house again. I'm not leaving you," Paul said, attempting to sit up in bed. "I kept thinking that I was going to die last night, or that Larry was going to—" he shook his head, shut his eyes against the awful thought. "What I asked you before, I know I said I'd wait, but we're getting married today. Now."

If what had just happened last night hadn't been so horrifying, Marian would've actually laughed at Paul, but there was nothing funny about what they had experienced and nothing funny about what motivated Paul to say what he was saying.

Again, he tried to rise up in bed, attempting to throw the blankets off of him and climb out.

"Paul. Paul!" Marian said. "Stop it!"

He settled some, looking drunken and drugged by the medication he was on, he stared, wobbly-eyed at her.

"I'm not playing, Marian. I'm serious. I love you. I love your kids, and everything that just happened made me realize just how much I need you all in my life. Marian," Paul said, taking her hand, holding it tight in his. "Will you marry me?"

At the cemetery, Marian watched as both Simone and Jabari silently said what they desired to their father after placing the flowers. Afterward they stepped back to take their place to her right.

Paul, standing to Marian's left, holding her hand, rubbing the stone on her wedding ring like he always did—the ring he placed on her finger the day they married two months ago—asked if there was anything Marian wanted to say.

She turned to Paul shocked, for until that moment, she had no intention of speaking a word to her ex-husband, and had no expectation of Paul asking her to. But she was quickly finding out that Paul was just that kind of man.

When it was time for Larry's funeral to be planned, Holy Sweet Spirit, the church Larry had founded, wanted to perform the services. They wanted it to be televised, wanted it open to the entire city of Atlanta.

"We want everyone who loved him, benefited from him and his teachings to be able to bid farewell to him," one of the deacons of the church told Marian. "We want it to be a joyous, wonderful occasion!"

That night, she paced her bedroom, shaking her head, waving her hands, proclaiming aloud that there was no way she would allow her husband to be seen as a hero, some great man of God when he was anything but.

"And why not?" Paul said. He sat across the room in his pajamas in a corner chair. "That's how most people saw him. If this would bring them some kind of joy, why take that from them?"

Marian turned, her mouth practically hanging open. "Because you know what he did."

"I know," Paul said, walking across the room to meet Marian. He took her by the shoulders. "But I also know if it wasn't him, I would've never been hired to be your assistant. We wouldn't be together right now."

"Paul, he had something to do with the death of your daughter."

Paul closed his eyes, exhaled deeply, and Marian could feel his hold on her tighten just a little. A moment later, he settled, his grip loosened, he opened his eyes and said, "Unfortunately, I lost my daughter long before Larry came around. I can't blame him entirely for that. There's some responsibility I own too."

"So you're telling me I should let them—"

"I'm not telling you anything, baby," Paul said, taking her face in his palms. "I'm just saying, your husband did enough bad while he was here, if someone wants to do something they think is good, why not let them?"

Marian allowed the ceremony. It was televised across Atlanta. The doors of Holy Sweet Spirit Baptist Church were opened for all who wished to come view Larry's body.

And they came.

The line of people, crying, fanning themselves in the hot Atlanta sun—falling to their knees, grief-stricken—stretched out the door, down the street and round the corner. There were on-the-street interviews by news teams, people saying how Bishop Larry Lakes changed their lives. There were tearful testimonials, how Christmas or Easter or New Years or their birthdays would've never been the same if it weren't for the Bishop.

That night, Marian lay in bed, Paul by her side, his arm around her, and watched some of that newscast, telling herself that was her final goodbye to her husband.

That was before Jabari decided he wanted to visit his father's gravesite, before Paul stood beside her, just a moment ago, and asked her if she had any words for her ex-husband.

"I...I don't think I have anything to that man," Marian told Paul, and for some reason she felt scared, as if her husband might've crawled right out of the ground, angry that she didn't want to speak to him.

"Fine. Then let's go," Paul said. "But if you're uncertain, if you think that maybe there's something you want to get off your chest once and for all."

Marian looked over her shoulder, then looked back to Paul, as if for help in deciding what to do.

Paul took the kid's hands. "C'mon, let's give your mother a little privacy."

Marian was left alone. She stared down on the headstone, and immediately felt herself filling with hate and rage, thinking of what Larry did to her son, the way he abused those boys, the times he hit her, cheated on her and—

"No!" Marian said, smearing the tears from her face with the palms of both her hands. She sniffled, shook her head, and again said, "No. You're gone. You can't hurt me or my children, or anyone else anymore. So I'm not going to bring myself down by hating you. I'm going to…I'm going to…thank you for…" Marian paused, the words coming hard for her, believing in some way her husband had gotten exactly what he deserved. But she also believed he wasn't born evil, just so mistreated, so neglected that one day he lost the battle he waged against becoming the man other men forced him to become.

He mentioned his abuse to her only one time, early in their marriage, as they lay together, facing one another after making love.

"My father…" Larry said, his eyes far off somewhere. "He would sell me to other men when I was a boy."

Marian lay shocked, her breath stopped in her chest, unable to believe what she heard.

"They would pay him to have sex with me. We were homeless a lot, and we needed money to survive. I guess I understood that," Larry said, his voice so low she almost couldn't hear it. "But I could never quite get why he would do that to me too. Why he would hold me down and do that to me too." His eyes were still glossy and unfocussed. "He said it was because he loved me. I don't know if that was true."

Staring down at her husband's grave, Marin pushed herself to remember the good her husband brought her.

"I want to thank you," she continued, "for loving me. Because even though you did horrible things, I believe love is a pure emotion, and you gave yours to me, and I thank you for that. And I want to thank you for the good you did for the people you helped, the people who loved you and always will. I want to thank you for the wonderful man you brought into my life," Marian said, turning to glance at Paul, who stood, still holding Jabari's and Simone's hands.

"Maybe in some way you knew you'd be leaving me, knew you weren't the good man you always claimed to be, and you wanted to make sure I got that good man I deserved. I don't know," Marian said, amazingly feeling a slight smile come to her face.

She turned back to look on Larry's grave.

"But most of all, Larry, I want to thank you for our two beautiful children, Jabari and Simone." She looked over her shoulder again, snuck a peak at her children, then turned back to the headstone.

"I'm sorry you felt I kept them from you, but I was only protecting them. Wherever you are now, I'm sure you understand that," Marian said, wiping at a fresh tear that managed to fall.

"I'm sorry that you had such a hard life, that you were treated so badly, but I'm thankful that you found me, that we had our family, and you were able to experience some joy and some peace with us. I hope that it took away some of your pain. I think that it might have," Marian said, lowering her head, feeling more tears fall from her eyes.

"And I'm thankful for that."

END—RMJ 5/29/14

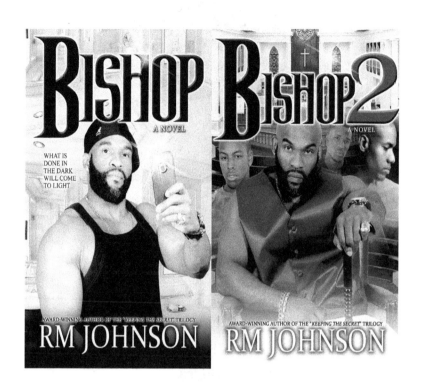

NOW AVAILABLE !!!

RM Johnson is the award-winning author of eighteen novels. They include the bestselling Harris Men series, The Million Dollar and The Keeping the Secret series. He holds an MFA in Creative Writing and currently resides, happily, in Atlanta, Georgia.

RM Johnson would love to hear your comments.

Email RM at **RMnovels@yahoo.com**

Please visit him at his website: **RM-Johnson.com**

Friend him at **Facebook.com/RMnovels**

Follow him at **Twitter.com/marcusarts**

CPSIA information can be obtained
at www.ICGtesting.com
Printed in the USA
BVHW042116020620
580815BV00016B/487